D1055295

zero and other fictions

Modern Chinese Literature from Taiwan

zero and other fictions

Huang Fan

edited and translated by John Balcom

COLUMBIA UNIVERSITY PRESS
NEW YORK

Columbia University Press wishes to express its appreciation for assistance given by the Chiang Ching-kuo Foundation for International Scholarly Exchange and Council for Cultural Affairs in the preparation of the translation and in the publication of this series.

Columbia University Press
Publishers Since 1893
New York   Chichester, West Sussex

Library of Congress Cataloging-in-Publication Data
   Huang, Fan, 1950–
   [Short stories. English. Selections]
   Zero and other fictions / Huang Fan ; edited and translated by John Balcom.
      p.   cm. — (Modern Chinese literature from Taiwan)
      ISBN 978-0-231-15740-7 (cloth : alk. paper) — ISBN 978-0-231-52805-4
(electronic)
   1. Taiwan—Fiction.   2. City and town life—Fiction.   3. Political fiction,
Chinese.   4. Satire, Chinese. I. Balcom, John. II. Title.

PL2865.F3A2   2011
895.1'352—dc22   2010051441

References to Internet Web sites (URLs) were accurate at the time of writing. Neither the author nor Columbia University Press is responsible for URLs that may have expired or changed since the manuscript was prepared.

contents

translator's preface

Huang Fan and Taiwan Fiction

Huang Fan, the literary phenomenon, is a bright star among Taiwan's so-called "new generation of writers," most of whom were born in the 1950s and who became prominent in the 1980s. Huang was such a prolific author during the 1980s that the decade is often referred to as the Age of Huang Fan. He has won every major literary award multiple times.

Huang Fan was born in Taipei in 1950. He grew up in straitened circumstances and was educated as an industrial engineer but held a variety of jobs, including food processing director and editor. After early success as an author, he turned to writing full-time.

He is known primarily as an urban writer, a political satirist, and a science fiction writer, but he is also widely considered one of the preeminent postmodernists from Taiwan. Critics tend to categorize Huang's work by period and by content. His writing has been divided into four periods:

Political and urban literature period, 1979–85. During this period, Huang focused on political and urban trends. "Lai Suo" is perhaps the most representative work from this period.

Postmodernist period, 1985–92. In this period, Huang's work, while retaining its focus on urban and political issues and science fiction, tended to include a metafictional level and often took an absurdist tone.

Reclusive period, 1993–2002. For almost a decade, Huang wrote little fiction. He spent a great deal of time studying Buddhism and writing essays.

Reemergence, 2003–present. Since 2003, Huang has reemerged as a major writer, penning two significant novels, *Impatient Country* (2003) and *College Thief* (2004), and a collection of shorter works, *Surmising Cat* (2005).

Regardless of how critics categorize Huang's writing, a number of consistent qualities unify the various periods and types of fiction, particularly his black humor and a critical spirit, often satirical in nature. Dr. Johnson said that in satire, wickedness or folly is censured. Huang's political and urban stories criticize recent trends; his science fiction, as might be expected, tends to censure human activity in a more generalized way; and even his postmodern fiction tends to satirize not only recent trends but also the act of writing itself.

The works included here were chosen as representative of Huang's oeuvre as a whole, and serve to illustrate the range of his creativity. Despite being a well-received writer in Taiwan, he has not been widely translated; this is the first collection of his work to appear in English.

Huang Fan burst onto the literary scene in 1979 with "Lai Suo," which was awarded the *China Times* Literary Prize. The story has been widely anthologized over the years and has gained the status of a modern classic. It portrays the pathos and absurdity of the eponymous victim of modern Taiwanese politics. Lai Suo's tragedy is that of a naïve individual who sees his few political ideals shattered and is himself used as a pawn by the more powerful in their drive for political control. The shifting time frame and stream-of-consciousness narration effectively convey Lai Suo's psychic dislocations against the backdrop of Taiwan's transition from Japanese colonial rule to the KMT White Terror, then to the economic takeoff on the 1970s.

The story was groundbreaking for a number of reasons. It was one of the first stories to transcend the strict political dichotomy by attacking both the ruling Nationalist (KMT) Party and the opposition. Also, the work is urban in focus. In terms of the history of the development of postwar fiction in Taiwan, this is important. Taiwan's great modernist writers had dealt with the entire spectrum of the Taiwan experience, but with an eye to aesthetic concerns. In the 1970s, there was a backlash against what many saw as the adverse Western influence on Taiwan literature, with a shift to Nativism and a greater concern for rural or proletarian content and themes. Huang's story directly challenges this position and restores some balance to the depiction of the Taiwan experience. Lai Suo, though a pathetic character himself, seems still to see himself as a cut above his wife's relatives from the countryside, who are coarse and naïve. The story contains the germ of much of Huang's later work.

"The Intelligent Man" was published in 1989. It is a satire-allegory about Taiwanese migration to the United States and the expansion of Taiwanese capital to mainland China and Southeast Asia in the 1980s, as well as the issues of cross-Strait relations and reunification. Yang Taisheng, the protagonist, is a rather typical example of Huang's urban characters (his name means Taiwan-born Yang). As Taiwan declines on the international stage in the 1970s, Yang leaves for the United States, where he first works in a restaurant and eventually is able to open his own furniture business in the Chinese enclave of Monterey Park. Later, as the Taiwanese in the States become more prosperous, they begin to long for traditional furnishings. Spurred by competition from a mainland furniture dealer, Yang branches out by importing more traditional furniture from Taiwan. In Taiwan he takes a second wife. Eventually, to stay competitive, Yang realizes that he needs to expand his production network to mainland China, where he takes another "wife." His other wives learn of this and demand a family meeting at a neutral site; Singapore is chosen for the mock unification talks. Once there, Yang, good businessman that he is, begins to scout out the possibilities.

Despite what might be termed the unreconstructed gender politics that inform the story, Huang has simply taken real-life accounts of Taiwanese businessmen with a wife in every port and produced an allegory in which the protagonist's "extended family" mirrors and satirizes the social-political trends of the day. The romanization systems I have used in the translation further underscore the political divisions among the Chinese.

Huang's "How to Measure the Width of a Ditch" marked a turn in his writing. Appearing in 1985, it is a key postmodernist text that is often seen as the inception point of the trend on the island. It is an absurdist metafictional piece in which writing itself comes under the author's critical eye. The story ostensibly deals with the narrator's reminiscences about his childhood in Taipei. As the plot develops, the reader relives the urban development of the city while being treated to an excursus into the nature of writing and the production of literature. The quirky, humorous text became a common feature of Huang's work and attracted a number of imitators.

In 1981, Huang published his first work of science fiction, *Zero*, which won the *United Daily News* Literary Prize in the novella category, the first work of science fiction to win a major literary award. It is a dystopian novel in the tradition of Orwell's *1984*—in fact, Huang's novella contains a sly reference to the earlier novel in that the author of a secret subversive text discovered by Xi De is named Winston. There is nothing decidedly Taiwanese about the story, even on the level of allegory; instead, Huang deals with the larger issues of totalitarianism and utopianism, the individual versus the collective, and the threat of a critical consciousness to a monolithic system.

When I first read the novel back in 1982, I was taken by its novelty within the Taiwan literary context. I think today we tend to forget the environment in which *Zero* was written and simply view it as just another bleak dystopian novel. In Taiwan, however, there was a burgeoning demand for political pluralism by a growing middle class, which was met with continued suppression; after all, Taiwan was still under martial law and one-party rule. For example, the Meilidao Incident of 1979 had occurred recently. Opposition political leaders, some associated with *Formosa Magazine*, held a pro-democracy demonstration in Kaohsiung to commemorate Human Rights Day. The demonstration was suppressed, the leaders arrested, and the magazine shut down. In subsequent months dozens of people were tried in military courts and given sentences ranging from two years to life in prison. The Lin family massacre occurred the following year, when the mother and two daughters of pro-democracy leader Lin Yi-hsiung, who was being held in prison, were murdered, even while under police protection. People who were critical of the ruling party were still being harassed, perhaps with fatal consequences. I recall the case of Chen Wen-Chen. After returning to Taiwan from the United States for a brief visit, the Carnegie-Mellon professor was questioned by security police. The next day his battered body was found on the National Taiwan University campus. The official explanation in the media was that he had committed suicide by leaping off a building, but most people on the street said he was pushed. In Taiwan's open society of today, many cannot recall the period when politics were discussed only in the privacy of one's home. Those closed, uncertain times formed the milieu in which Huang wrote his first work of science fiction.

In *Zero*, there is a flattening of life, reducing it to a politically correct sort of conformity in which all individualism is discouraged. Most people stay on the straight and narrow, but the main character, Xi De, is different. (With his inquiring and skeptical mind, he is not unlike the writer in contemporary society.) From very early he is fascinated by the Dark Ages, the time before the new world order was established. This leads to discussions with an elderly history teacher. Xi De begins to doubt aspects of the official story and continues to observe things with a quiet skepticism. Eventually he discovers a hidden text by one of the early founders of the new order, and his doubts grow. Soon he is recruited by a revolutionary group that seeks to overthrow the totalitarian state. His rebel activities come to an end when he is captured and executed. In Huang's novel, even individualism and revolt are manipulated by the totalitarian system, the control of which is so absolute that it includes its own opposition. It tempts, and then destroys those who succumb. The novella is probably Huang's science fiction at its bleakest. His later science fiction works contain a heavy infusion of a postmodernist sensibility.

Huang Fan has had a tremendous impact upon the landscape of contemporary fiction in Taiwan. This is perhaps less apparent today, thirty years since he began writing. Through the critical lens of his fiction, with its political and urban content, he was a driving force in the pluralism that became the byword of Taiwan literature in the 1980s. The island's growing educated middle class was demanding more openness and liberalization. Pushing genre boundaries coincided with and encouraged further movement in that direction in society. It is hoped that this small selection of his work conveys just a little of his creative genius.

JB
Middlebury/Monterey

acknowledgments

I would like to thank the following individuals and organizations. First, my heartfelt gratitude to David Wang for supporting this project and to Jennifer Crewe for making this book a reality. I would also like to thank my editor at Columbia University Press, Leslie Kriesel, for another fine job. Thanks also, as always, to my wife, Yingtsih, for her assistance and for her translation of "The Intelligent Man." I also offer a tip of the hat to the anonymous readers of this book for their useful suggestions and comments. I would also like to acknowledge the support of the Chiang Ching-kuo Foundation for International Scholarly Exchange and Council for Cultural Affairs as well as *The Chinese PEN*, in which "The Intelligent Man" first appeared.

lai suo

Mr. Han's face appeared on television, tired and dignified. It was June 24, 1978. No importance was given to the usual disorder in the world that day, nor was any new significance bestowed upon it. But for Lai Suo, who sat properly in front of the television and whose expression was by turns one of anger, depression, and pensiveness, it was the start of a series of losses and confusion run amok through time.

How to explain this?

After his initial agitation had passed, Lai Suo entered his bedroom, crying and tearing his hair. His wife stood at the locked door and called his name, but there was no response, so she went back to her cleaning. She liked to hose down everything in sight.

In the summer of 1979, Lai Suo, who was bare from the waist up and lying in bed in his apartment next to the freeway, discovered that his wife with her big butt, who was lying on her side next to him, was snoring away, whistling like a tea kettle. Throwing his robe over his shoulders, he stood on the balcony, looking up at the star-filled sky, peering into the dreamlike past and the unknown future. Only when the first light of morning from the east shone on his half-bald head, which resembled an egg, did he return to that time when he sat in front of the television in 1978—the beginning, end, and intermission in his life.

1

One week after getting out of prison, Lai Suo turned thirty. He wore an old gray woolen suit, was as thin as a matchstick (he had contracted a chronic stomach ailment), and had pronounced crow's feet at his eyes. His gaze never moved from his feet in order to avoid the looks of others. He stood in front of the desk of his older brother, the jam manufacturer.

"I can do any job; I won't make any trouble."

"Never mind, Ah Suo, I'm your brother."

He didn't meet his brother's sympathetic, caring eyes, for they always sent him scampering away in fright like a rat. In point of fact, he was indeed nothing more than a rat. He'd ratted on his fellow prisoners to make himself even more like a rat. At the age of twenty-one, as he stood before the presiding judge of the military tribunal, he once acted like a man. Impassioned, he mumbled his point and even shed tears. But the outcome wasn't quite what he had in mind, mainly because he was just an insignificant little person. He had stood at the university gate handing out mimeographed flyers, stammering the lines written on them. His strange manner had attracted the attention of the students coming and going, and they were soon laughing. As the laughter sounded, Mr. Han and a number of important subordinates were setting foot on Japanese soil. Several days later he rented a house on a secluded street in the Ginza district. After everything was taken care of, Mr. Han began storing up a great deal of sperm for his four future mixed-blood kids, much like collecting materials for the speech he gave on TV that day in 1978 upon returning home to the motherland.

Mr. Han was the very last person he worshipped. Later he learned not to worship any living soul because they all would die. The way he saw it was that the great would die, the stupid would die, and so too would he. Upon death, no one, regardless of who they were, seemed bad. Before Du Ziyi died, when he cut a fart, his face would swell and take on the color of pork liver before he released a miserable little tweeter. Du, whose head was filled with nothing but Communism, believed that Marx was something intermediate between man and god. For this reason, he would say to those with no education: "Divvy up the money of the rich"; to intellectuals he would say: "Class struggle is the impetus of social progress"; and to himself he would say: "Have no regrets." But Du never once shared the food his family brought when they visited him in prison. He was a fat guy with a big round face, the spitting image of what he called the petite bourgeoisie. Just before dying, Du clutched his cell-mate, with whom he had shared hardship and misfortune, and said, "Never believe anyone."

Lai Suo never forgot those words. As he lay in bed, recalling the past, Mr. Han, Fatso, the Japanese, and the stern-looking judge, his tears once again began to fall.

"Don't bother your dad," he heard his wife, who was standing by the door, say to their twelve-year-old daughter.

"Why is he making such strange noises in his sleep?"

"He is not feeling well."

A little while later, he got out of bed and went to the bathroom to wash up. The bathroom was always immaculate. Distorted faces were reflected in the squeaky-clean mosaic tiles (facing the wall, he shook his head). The faces moving on the tiles metamorphosed in unpredictable ways, suddenly a toothy grin, eyebrows suddenly falling out and chin stretching, nostrils suddenly pointing upward, revealing a walnut-sized Adam's apple. "I've become thin." He sighed. He stood on the scale next to the bathtub to weigh himself. The needle stopped at 46. It was the same as last month's record. But last month he had not worn a stitch of clothing. He had squat-ted naked on the scale while singing, "Sitting alone at night beneath the lamp, a cold wind blows over. . . ." He had sung only half the verse when his wife knocked on the door. "Ah Suo, what are you doing in there?" He threw open the door and his wife let out a piercing scream, and, looking quickly right and left, scolded, "You're going to die!" So now when he took off his pants and crouched on the scale, the needle spun reluctantly backward for a moment. Stepping naked off the scale, he sat on the toilet; the wet toilet seat made him shiver, sending a chill up his spine, where it bored deep into the base of his skull. Immediately he returned to the day on which he got married in 1963.

2

The bride's face was heavily powdered, her hair permed in ringlets. Her large backside indicated that she would later bear a great number of progeny for the groom. The wedding reception that day went smoothly, and the big gold "double-happiness" character in the hall added to the atmosphere. The bride's parents and her two brothers had come up from the distant countryside. Out of politeness, her brothers, who were chewing betel nut, spit the betel-nut juice into napkins, which littered the floor. Ah Suo's elder brother was very excited and went from table to table with his wine cup in hand, offering toasts. His face was flushed. At that moment, he suddenly announced to all assembled that he was giving several shares of stock in his jam company to his brother. The friends and relatives applauded. He wasn't drunk when he uttered these words. There were only two tables at the reception, and two of the seats were empty— they had been reserved for two important relatives, but they were unable to attend.

After the guests had left, Lai Suo quickly got under the covers, where he set to work stripping his bride bare. He was so intent on what he was doing that he forgot to turn off the nightstand lamp on which had been pasted the character for "happiness." For this reason, the bride did her best, twisting and turning, looking here and there.

"Oh!" she shouted. "This is such a pretty room."

"Hold still," said Lai Suo, "or I'll never be able to get this button undone."

In addition to undoing buttons, he could also thread a needle, sew a hem, and do calisthenics, all of which he had learned in prison. This morning, fifteen years later, he suddenly bent down and tried to touch his toes. Despite his exertions, he couldn't reach that spot twenty centimeters below his knees with his fingers. He was wearing a pair of shorts from which protruded his scrawny legs. His kneecaps looked like hard tumors. Lai Suo's wife stared at him uncomprehendingly.

"When I was young, I could touch this," he squatted and patted the floor, "my palms flat, without bending my knees."

"What's so good about that?"

Nothing at all, so forget it. At that moment he was standing absent-mindedly in front of the filter in the jam plant. The needle of the pressure gauge was steadily rising. The motor below was screeching. The syrup entered the filter, which looked like a bomb, through a pipe in one end and came out a pipe in the other end. Then it flowed precipitously into a condenser suspended in the air, emerging from which it was no longer syrup but rather a mass of shiny, gelatinous substance. The whole process was reminiscent of that used by God when he made man. Perhaps there are those who would say that a fetus takes shape from the blood concentrated in the womb.

But that is not what Lai Suo's mother thought. At only seven months, he was in a hurry to leave his mother's belly, bawling in a world that was not yet ready to receive him. His mother, whose face was pale, lay to one side while his father stood, in only a military undershirt, continuously wringing his hands, his head covered with sweat. A drop of sweat fell on the tip of the infant's nose—this is humanity's earliest recorded impression of falling rain. There were some other people standing around the bed as well.

"What are we going to do? What are we going to do?" Lai Suo's father kept muttering.

"Oh no! Why is his skin blue?" asked his second maternal aunt, who later had a son who worked for the American military advisers and therefore was absent from the wedding banquet.

"My son?" his mother said, closing her eyes. "Let me hold him."

"You can't hold him yet," replied the midwife. "He has to be wrapped in medicated cloth; otherwise he might change shape."

It was most likely on account of the medication that he became uglier as he grew, reaching adolescence late at sixteen years of age. But adolescence wasn't all that troublesome for him. He was the smallest in his class and sat only a meter from the podium. The Japanese teacher was constantly but furtively scratching his crotch. He suffered from eczema but didn't think anyone could see, He was wrong.

"*Zhina* (China)!" said the Japanese. "All of you, repeat after me."

"Cheena," said Lai Suo.

"Do you all know that you are not Chinese but Taiwanese?"

"But Teacher," replied one local student, "my grandfather said that we all came from China with Koxinga."

"Bastard," swore the Japanese. The teacher's saliva hit Lai Suo in the face, and when he raised his hand to wipe it off he discovered a pimple.

As the pimples began to grow, some began to fester. He was walking down the street in Dadaocheng, squeezing pimples as he walked, his face filling with red and white blotches. As he squeezed the fifth one, his companion, Little Lin, elbowed him.

"Hurry, look!" Little Lin whispered. "Isn't that Tanaka Ichiro?"

"Who is Tanaka Ichiro?"

"The Japanese guy who taught us history two years ago."

Both sides of the street were filled with straw mats, on which knelt Japanese with their heads bowed. All kinds of things were spread out on the mats, including costume jewelry, fans, high military boots, and dolls dressed in kimonos. Lai Suo had just turned eighteen and the Japanese had surrendered not long before that. At first the locals didn't know what to do. Lai Suo's father, who worked for the Japanese, was only able to collect himself several months later. He rented a house near the Central Market and got into the fruit business. Fruits are good to eat but troublesome plants. During the day, Lai Suo would push a handcart along the Danshui River, where he would establish several bases of operation. Since he didn't possess a hawker's voice, he'd always sit on a cushion at the head of the cart with his bare feet in a basket, where he would absentmindedly rub the watermelons the size of human heads. In the evening, he put on a pair of noisy wooden clogs and sauntered around.

"Thank you, thank you, *arigato*, *arigato*." The Japanese would bow at the waist until their heads nearly touched the ground.

"Let's go and say 'thank you' and see if he recognizes us."

Lai Suo thought about it for a moment.

"No, that's not nice."

"Why?"

Lai Suo thought some more.

But something prevented him from thinking and forced him back five, ten, twenty years. . . .

"Is there something wrong with the machine, Mr. Lai?"

"Is there something wrong with the machine, Mr. Lai?" asked the factory worker again.

"What did you say? Oh, the pressure seems a bit high."

"There are too many impurities this time making it difficult to filter. Listen to the motor."

It was not just the motor. The sounds of the mixer, pump, and steam valve all converged into a mighty torrent of noise.

Lai Suo pricked up his ears and listened.

3

He seemed to hear a number of other sounds. His two maple-leaf ears were completely exposed to the continuous noise on the street—buses, trucks, cabs, motorcycles, as well as the occasional siren of an ambulance as it rushed by. All of these sounds knocked on Lai Suo's eardrums as if they wanted to penetrate even deeper, but were stopped in the middle by something—it was like an acoustic tile on which was inscribed: LAI SUO, TAIPEI, JUNE 1978, TRAVELER THROUGH TIME AND SPACE.

At the time, he was riding home on the bus. The driver treated his bus like a toy and had the radio on at full volume. The speaker was right above his head. Lai Suo was curled up on the green plastic seat when a large, middle-aged woman sat down next to him. She was fierce looking, her two breasts cascaded down, and she smelled of cheap perfume. His wife used Max Factor, which he could recognize immediately. On the back of the seat in front of him, someone had scrawled several words with an eyebrow pencil: "Lonely? Call Li Meihua at 871–3042." Lai Suo smiled to himself.

The bus stopped in front of the city office building. Lai Suo sat gazing as the receding scenery came to a halt. Several seconds later, the scenery once again began to recede. The pedestrians, gray trees, dirty houses, and long billboards all seemed as if they were being swallowed in an incomparably large mouth. As the bus crossed an overpass, Lai Suo shut his eyes for a while. When he opened them again, he was standing in the reception room of *Pan-Asia Magazine* in front of a full-length mirror. A small guy with a bland look on his face appeared in the mirror. The door opened suddenly and an office worker poked his head in.

"Mr. Han would like you to go to the meeting room."

"What for? I'm here to pick up my pay and then leave."

"He wants you to go, so you'd better go."

"It was agreed that I was to pick up my money each day."

"Stop with the nonsense."

He didn't recognize anyone except Mr. Han and the office worker who led him in. Mr. Han smiled when he saw him. He quickly lowered his head and shamefully looked at the dirty soles of his feet. Stepping on the clean *tatami* mats, the office worker shook his head with loathing and said, "It's okay, step up."

"Lai Suo!" Mr. Han stepped over and clapped him on the shoulder. "This is Mr. Chen and Mr. Lin. Have a seat. And this is Mr. Huang."

"How long have you worked here?"

"Four months."

"What did you do before you came here?"

"I sold fruit by the Danshui River."

"Why aren't you still selling?" said Mr. Han as he turned to the gentlemen sitting cross-legged on the *tatami* mats. "All business is doing badly."

"I wasn't any good at it," replied Lai Suo. "I sometimes gave incorrect change and my voice isn't very good."

"Okay. You went to school, right? How would you like to be a regular office worker?"

The gentlemen looked up and eyed him. One whispered to another, "A simple, honest fellow."

Lai Suo heard him.

A simple, honest fellow. What does that mean? On the bus thirty years later, Lai Suo listened attentively to the voices. The bus passed down a stretch of road where water pipe was being laid. Sawhorses, concrete water pipes, and excavators were piled on both sides of the road. He didn't know how many times altogether the city had dug up and repaired the road around the municipal building. But that had nothing whatsoever to do with him. Besides, everyone ought to have something to do, something at least to keep himself busy. The woman with the big breasts was yanking fiercely on the bell cord, her bottom half pressing heavily on his shoulder. Lai Suo couldn't help but throw her an angry look. The bell rang for quite a while before the woman finally sat down. A shadow passed in front of Lai Suo. He quickly turned to look out the window; the bus was now proceeding along a smooth, gray, monotonous highway. The scenery outside continued to recede into that large and fierce-looking maw. Lai Suo persisted with his deep, unending meditations.

"What does a regular office worker do?" he heard himself ask in his heart.

"The work is lighter and you take home an additional 100 *yuan* a month."

"Why?" he asked himself again.

"Take a look at this," said Mr. Han, handing him a thin sheaf of papers. "Sign your name at the bottom, and bring your seal tomorrow and affix it."

Lai Suo read the first few lines.

"I vow to join the Taiwan Democratic Progressive Alliance under the leadership of Mr. Han Zhiyuan and to do my utmost for my fellow Taiwanese. . . . If I violate this oath, may Heaven have no mercy."

4

Lai Suo kept on asking himself until he was exhausted. He got off the bus and started toward home. On the way, he stopped at a bakery where he purchased a large bag of peanuts and three lollipops. He could eat the peanuts on the balcony that night, and there was one lollipop for each of the kids. This one was chocolate, according to the clerk, and this one was cream, and this one was lemon. These are five-spice peanuts. What else do you want, Sir? Nothing, nothing else. But what about Lai Suo's wife? She didn't seem to need anything. She had everything and nothing. Sometimes Lai Suo was confused. How could anyone have a wife like his, with her energy, who always seemed on the verge of exploding, and who would hose down everything at any moment? She insisted that everyone in the family put on clean clothes each day. She patiently went through their pockets. "There's no end to the dirty things," she said. "If I'm not careful, I might pull out a rat one day." As she finished speaking, she tossed Lai Suo's hankie into the washing machine. Her aim was good—socks, ties, towels, and the little yellow school caps worn by the kids. Lai Suo shook his head, and as he stepped on the wet floor, he slid into the living room.

Although his wife was that way, thought Lai Suo, at least he could stand it, even including what happened in the deep of night; he could take it all.

When he was half asleep, she would roll over on him without any prior warning and press him under her corpulent body. Lai Suo would use every ounce of strength to free himself from the nightmare. He struggled, crowing strangely.

"Ah Suo, I rolled over on you again," his wife said, deeply apologetic.

"That's okay," was how Lai Suo, who had been married only a matter of months, replied.

"Did I hurt you?"

"A little," he replied. "I have a bad dream every time."

"What dream?"

"It's very weird."

At that time, Lai Suo was standing on the floor of his prison cell, facing the wall and crying. Cold, dim rays of sunlight entered his cell through the small window above his head, falling on the soles of Fatso Du's swinging bare feet. Du frequently scratched his toes while narrowing his eyes to fix his gaze on the weeping Lai Suo. Lai Suo had just received news of his mother's death. She had visited him once a month in prison, bringing him things to eat and leaving with tear-swollen eyes. Lai Suo heard the news from the other side of the mesh in the prison visiting room. He couldn't help but howl. Clenching his fists, he struck the mesh like a desperate rat until the guards came and pulled him away. His older brother wept gently on the other side of the mesh. Lai Suo walked unsteadily into his cell. Fatso Du grabbed the small box of food items from Lai Suo and had soon stuffed himself. In a good mood now, he thought about saying a few words of comfort.

"Save your strength," said Fatso. "You still have six years and four months to cry."

Lai Suo abruptly stood up, turned, and eyed him, his shoulders heaving.

"What did you say?"

"I said save your strength. What good does it do to cry?"

"Fuck your mother!"

The next minute, Lai Suo and Fatso were rolling around on the floor. In another thirty seconds, Lai Suo was pinned under his enormity. Lai Suo struggled, kicking and shouting, his spit flying, covering Fatso's face.

"Keep on screaming and I'll crush you to death."

He calmed down only at this show of malicious ferocity.

"Sometimes I dream of my mom," said Lai Suo to his wife, who was lying beside him.

5

It was already very late and Lai Suo, who was in a good mood, was still sitting on the balcony shelling peanuts, his two legs propped up on the railing. It was the beginning of summer and the stars shimmered on the horizon and a line of headlights shone on the freeway. Lai Suo, wearing a BVD undershirt, took up the responsibility of trying to solve the riddle of life. His expression was by turns warm, cold, and confused. He was busy shelling peanuts, which he picked up between thumb and forefinger and then squeezed, making the peanut pop, revealing the white peanuts inside the shell. Lai Suo threw the shells down into the street. With the help of a breeze, peanut shells littered the entire street.

"What's wrong with having a drink?" asked Lai Suo's dad.

"You could end up with illnesses such as congestion of the brain, rheumatism, or an ulcer," said Lai Suo's mom.

Lai Suo took his feet down off the railing and changed his position as he continued to hear the squabbling among the dead.

"I'm in a bad mood."

"So what?"

Lai Suo's dad worked very hard. He was more or less illiterate and he wasn't very strong, but he had a family to support. During the day he worked in a malt sugar plant that supplied the Japanese military. Bare-chested, Lai Suo's dad would jump up on a large metal vat that was filled with glutinous rice powder and a great deal of water. He would vigorously stir the contents of the vat with a wooden paddle not unlike an oar. The sweat would drip off of him like rain into the vat. After half an hour, he would add a bucket of green malt, cooking the mixture over a coal fire. Then Lai Suo's dad would jump to another vat that contained the syrup produced the night before. He stirred the syrup until it emitted steam, and only then would he jump down. Jumping up on and down off the vats dozens of times each day had made his legs quite muscular, though his upper body remained as scrawny as ever.

"Ah Yun can help make some money right away," said Lai Suo's mom, taking away the bottle. "Ah Suo is smarter, so let him stay in school."

"What good does it do to go to school?" replied Lai Suo's dad.

"You are at a disadvantage because you had no schooling."

"Mom, you always wanted me to go to school," interrupted Lai Suo on the balcony, "but maybe Dad was right."

"Why am I so disadvantaged?" said Lai Suo's dad angrily. "With no money, I get no respect. I ought to have done with it."

"I haven't had a good day since I married you." Lai Suo's mom was also angry. "All you can do is drink, drink away any good opportunity."

"Did Ah Quan"—Ah Quan was a distant relative who tried to get Lai Suo's dad to go to Taipei to do business—"tell you if he is making money?"

"Not right now, but the future's uncertain."

"We can talk about the future later."

Lai Suo's dad should see Ah Quan today. He wears a 20,000-*yuan* suit and drives a Mercedes-Benz. His dyed hair is black and oily, and though over 60 years of age, he still leers lasciviously at the little butts of the nightclub hostesses in their hot pants.

"Ah Suo will one day amount to a good deal more than you."

"That's his business."

Lai Suo's dad finally gave in and agreed to let their son study in public school. He even bought him a pair of sneakers to wear to school, which no doubt cost a pretty penny. On rainy days, Lai Suo would walk barefoot and carry his shoes.

"Don't think I'll be buying things for you," threatened Lai Suo's dad. "If you do badly in school, I'll give you a beating."

"Why scare the child?"

"I work hard to make money with no thought of my age."

What was the point in bringing up all this? In the end, Lai Suo became furious, stood up, and in a rage hurled the remaining peanuts down onto the street. He walked into the living room, where his children were sitting in front of the television.

"We finished our homework a long time ago, Dad."

"Your mom?"

"She went to bed."

Not wishing to wake his wife, Lai Suo gently closed the door. He was exhausted today and had something to do the following day. Yep, tomorrow he had to take the day off, because his cousin was ill and in Xu Hospital. His cousin's wife had called and said that his cousin was always thinking of sneaking out (he had another woman outside whom he hadn't been in touch with for several days and was certainly very worried). As a result, she decided to hide his leather shoes; after all, she figured if he dared to go out on the street in his pajamas and slippers, she might as well admit defeat and have done with it. What else could she do? Listening on his end of the phone, Lai Suo shook his head without replying. Why should he get mixed up in other people's business, especially when he had more important things to do? He had to go see Mr. Han—it had been thirty-six hours since his face appeared on the television news. As far as he was concerned, that stretch of time was equal to several decades for other people. Therefore he had to make things clear. But what exactly did he have to make clear? Who could say after such a long time? He had three children and Mr. Han was nearly seventy, an age by which some people have false teeth. Had he heard the joke about dentures? Perhaps he should just shake his hand and say, "Mr. Han, it's been a long time."

"Ah Suo, why have you been sitting alone on the balcony for so long?"

His wife had not gone to sleep. She was wearing pink Triumph-brand underwear; her entire body exuded a fragrant warmth. She had used this method, among others, to have three children by him as well as to buy two houses at government auction. When her relatives from the country came to Taipei, she would take them out on the town to listen to music and eat in restaurants. The country people were stunned by the imposing style of the city and would be left speechless, their mouths hanging open. At such times, Lai Suo's wife was always excited and her tone of voice was unusually tender, making eyes at Lai Suo, who looked helpless. That night Lai Suo's wife would be overly enthusiastic. She was nearly forty with a fat belly, but laughed and shouted like a young girl and crushed Lai Suo under her nearly sixty kilos till he could scarcely breathe.

"I'm eating peanuts."

"Peanuts cause too much internal heat," she said. "You have been acting strangely the last few days. What's going on?"

"I've had a lot on my mind," said Lai Suo, lying down. "Oh yeah, tomorrow I won't be going to the factory—I'm going to the hospital to see my cousin Ah Zong."

"Why do you want to go see him? He has to disturb others with the slightest little illness. What's with him anyway?" She didn't like Lai Suo's family. "Well, I'm not going—I have a pile of laundry to wash tomorrow."

"Okay," replied Lai Suo, breathing a sigh of relief. "I want to go to bed a little early."

But his wife wasn't going to let him off so easily. She pressed closer to Lai Suo and he could smell the heavy, hot fragrance of her body.

"Do you remember when we first met?"

"Yeah (mmm)."

"You told me I was nice."

"Yeah (mmm)."

"The first time you kissed me, you wanted me to close my eyes. Do you remember?"

"Yeah," said Lai Suo, "yeah, yeah."

6

At that time, the Taipei-bound bus stopped in the middle of the bridge. The Danshui River, which was always dirty, flowed below. At the head of the bridge a black-and-white police car was stopped. Squeezed in among the passengers on the rush-hour bus, Lai Suo, dressed in his Sunday best, looked as if he were suffering. "Those who want to get off, move forward; the rest of you, don't block the door," said the female bus conductor angrily. "Why do you just stand there?" Lai Suo didn't reply until they were in front of the Shiji Restaurant: "I, I want to get off here."

Lai Suo did in fact get off the bus and bought a basket of apples by the roadside. The apples looked as if they had just been taken out of cold storage, but a sick patient probably wouldn't notice the deep purple tone. Ah Zong would say that it was enough for him to come and he shouldn't have brought the apples. His cousin, who was sixty, still had a ruddy face. Every day he got up at five or six and went to Beitou to soak in the hot springs, after which he would walk to his mistress's house at the foot of the mountain for breakfast. When he returned home, his wife would be bustling about in the kitchen and Ah Zong would walk gingerly up behind her and slap her rump. His wife would shout and his cousin would say, "What's cooking for today?" with an innocent expression on his face.

A little while later, Lai Suo placed the basket of apples on the floor of the phone booth across the street from the seven-floor Xu Hospital. Just then there was no activity at the hospital door; if the patients weren't all asleep, then they must have all died. Lai Suo hadn't had time to find out when the doctors arrived for work, when the patients got up, or if they had breakfast upon rising in the morning. He opened the phone book, which was three centimeters thick, and ran his finger over it.

"Is that the TV station?"

"That's right," said a young woman, yawning.

"Are you doing an interview with Mr. Han like the papers said?"

"You've got the wrong number—this is the dining hall. You should call the information desk."

"But you ought to know if Mr. Han Zhiyuan is going to be there."

"What Han Zhiyuan? It's either the arts program or the soap opera," the girl said, becoming impatient. "I know all the famous singers and movie stars here. What does your Han Zhiyuan do? Don't you know the number of the information desk?"

"He, he just returned from Japan."

"That's strange. The only one who just came back from Japan is Deng Lijun. Let me give you the number for the information desk."

"Thanks!" said Lai Suo, as he deposited a one *yuan* coin and dialed the number.

"Hello, Information Desk," said Lai Suo, before the other party could say anything.

"Hello, Information Desk," said the girl at the desk.

"Is Mr. Han Zhiyuan doing an interview at your station this evening?"

"Yes. It's on *Newsmakers* tonight at eight o'clock. Don't you take the *TV Guide*?"

"No," said Lai Suo, "but I would like to get a copy."

"You can call this number," said the girl. "Tell them that Miss Ma at the TV station referred you. Don't forget. That way you won't miss a program like *Newsmakers*. Is there anything else?"

Not bad, the girl was doing his work for him. Receiver in hand, Lai Suo chuckled with his back to the door of the phone booth. Lai Suo had a way of dealing with salespeople (newspapers, magazines, soy sauce, makeup). He listened patiently to the end of their lengthy spiels (he even looked as if he had been sold), then he would coldly bring everything to a halt: "You have a point, but we already subscribe, we already have it, I have always used that brand."

"Thank you," Lai Suo finally said. "I'll be sure to call and tell them that Miss Ma at the TV station referred me. Do I get any preferential treatment?"

7

Lai Suo stepped out of the phone booth. The hospital on the other side of the street appeared to be coming to life. Several people came out of the hospital door and looked in all directions. A taxicab pulled up and stopped in front, and two people got out—the first patient of the day. From his side of the restless street, Lai Suo couldn't tell which of the two was ill. Those who had looked up and down the street got into the cab.

The driver turned to look at them before they were gone in a flash. Lai Suo stood at the side of the street, but with no break in the traffic, he had to head back down the sidewalk to the traffic signal forty of fifty meters away. The sidewalk was planted with acacias fenced off with an iron railing. Under the trees stood a Taipei municipal trashcan in the shape of a bird on which was written: "I love to eat fruit peels and paper scraps." Lai Suo searched his pockets but couldn't find anything to stuff in the bird's mouth. I love to eat fruit peels and paper scraps, repeated Lai Suo to himself, we all love to eat fruit peels and paper scraps.

The traffic light suddenly turned green, and Lai Suo hurried across the street to the red brick sidewalk on the other side. The hard rubber soles of his leather shoes were perfect for the streets of Taipei. As to the streets of Taipei—when it was put to a municipal official, he said that his idea was simply to drop an atomic bomb on the buildings and start over. It was a joke! But back to the original topic, Lai Suo's leather shoes with their thick rubber soles positively shone in the morning light, and they went with his good suit and the red brick sidewalk.

He arrived at the hospital only after taking the long way around.

The nurse wearing glasses at the reception desk looked as if she had just woken up. She eyed the basket of apples Lai Suo had placed on the desk, and said, "What is your relationship to the patient in room 201?"

"Cousin."

"Those are nice shoes," said the nurse, poking her head out. "Too bad they're too small."

"My shoes are too small?"

She shrugged her shoulders.

"Would you like an apple?"

"Thanks," said the nurse, "but I've already eaten. Take the elevator on the right."

He could hear his cousin Ah Zong's voice through the door of his room. It was a voice filled with pleading, threats, curses, and suppressed anger.

"Okay! But when can I get out of the hospital?" he asked.

"The doctor says you'll be released when you're released," his wife replied.

"Doctor!"

Lai Suo pushed open the door. His appearance put an end to their bickering. Lai Suo, who had been sitting in a Western-style restaurant near the television station waiting for his food, clearly recalled what had just transpired. At that time he had pressed his face to the brown smoked-glass window, wondering what was going on outside. It was gloomy outside—the pedestrians and cars resembled floating spirits. But what had happened to the sun behind him when he pushed open the door and came in? Perhaps it had died. Lai Suo moved his face away from the window (a passerby had glanced at the window—obviously he couldn't see inside, because he fixed his hair facing Lai Suo). He couldn't stand the stupid look of the fellow. How much better it would be if the windows were blue or green. You'd suddenly find yourself standing on a vast golf course, hitting a green ball into a green hole; then you'd widen your green eyes and lift your green leg. . . .

"Ah Suo, you arrived in the nick of time," said his cousin as he excitedly scurried back and forth on the blue carpet in his bare feet. He was wearing a pair of silk pajamas and his puffy face was all red. His fleshy belly and double chin wiggled constantly.

"You tell me who is sick," he said, out of breath, "you tell me who's sick."

If you're not sick, what are you doing in the hospital? Lai Suo, who had been sitting in the restaurant, smiled happily to himself.

"Ah Suo, not only has your cousin not recovered from his illness, but his nerves are being affected," said his wife, pointing at his head. "Just look at his crazy behavior."

They kept on bickering. Lai Suo got tired of standing so sat down on the sofa, placing the apples he'd brought to one side.

"Have an apple, you two."

"Great, Ah Suo, shut him up with an apple."

"What do you mean by that?" raged Ah Zong, sitting in bed. "Not only won't she let me put on my shoes or make a phone call, but she also insists that I shut my mouth."

"Look at how anxious he is," said his wife, taking a seat. Lai Suo looked at them sympathetically. He wanted to say something, but he wasn't in the mood. He had something important to take care of—he would soon go to the restaurant to eat and wait, wait as long as necessary.

The lunch hour had passed and Lai Suo was still sitting there. He wanted to do something. Perhaps he should call home, but his wife would ask too many questions. She'd want to know what was happening in Taipei (she had been there only the week before). What were those loose women wearing? Was the supermarket offering a 20 percent discount? If so, he should bring something home. But what? It didn't matter. It would just be a knotty problem for him, and that was something he didn't want, at least not now—today he couldn't take the risk. He wanted to go and see Mr. Han. He had to get ready. He wanted to be radiant with well-being and wanted to talk with confidence and composure; otherwise, why was he dressed in his best suit?

In terms of clothes, Lai Suo was dressed not nearly so nicely when he got married. The Lai family had never thought much of dressing up. "Eating your fill is the most important thing," Lai Suo's dad had taught them. "If you have money, you don't have to buy this or that; when disaster comes and you have to flee, can you eat your clothes?" Lai Suo's dad seemed to be fleeing throughout his entire life and had been scared witless by the American bombers. He lived to seventy-two, when his heart gave out in a special ward in the Veterans Hospital. Before he died the ward was quiet, save for the purr of the air conditioner in the window. At that time, even the roar of a 747 overhead was inaudible in the hospital.

8

Perhaps he really was sleeping. That head of his that had experienced so much anxiety and distress was leaning back against the Naugahyde booth under the soft, feeble light of the restaurant. Two sunken cheeks, a few strands of gray hair hanging over his forehead (his bald head, dull), sagging wrinkles, and pale, dry lips. That was the real Lai Suo. Lai Suo, whose inner strength was nearly exhausted; Lai Suo, who had been born as a member of the human race, glorious, progressive, cooperative, and favored, awake or sleeping, sad or happy (he laughed like a bashful young girl), had deeply experienced the seven emotions and the six sensory pleasures.

At the sound of a voice speaking through a microphone, he opened his eyes.

"Ladies and gentlemen, tonight's show is about to get under way."

To his surprise, Lai Suo discovered people seated at the nearby tables. The show was starting at six o'clock. Goodness! He had spent the whole afternoon sitting there; a whole afternoon and he hadn't done a thing except sit there. He was about to meet Mr. Han. At that historic moment, he wasn't prepared at all. He ought to at least say something, like the words spoken by Mr. Han at the airport—brief, apropos, and filled with emotion. He must have prepared a draft before boarding the plane and revised it while flying over the Pacific. Finally, when the cabin door opened, he adjusted his tie and cleared his throat.

"Sir, would you care for something to drink?" asked the waitress.

"Anything is fine, maybe a coffee."

Although time was short, the TV station across the street could be reached by an underground pedestrian walkway in five minutes. He'd have to pay his bill ten minutes before and with five minutes in the bathroom, he'd have just enough time. He didn't have to draft a long speech—Mr. Han would remember him and would even grasp his hand excitedly, and with tears streaming down his face, he would apologize to Lai Suo and for the rest of his life would regret that incident. So, even though he would say this, what would Lai Suo do? He'd best just bear his misfortune; besides, he was already used to it.

"Ladies and gentlemen, I want to sing a song for you."

The light fell on a long-haired young man with a broad nose and a yellow face. Holding a guitar, the young man began to croon. He sang a song in English. Eyes narrowed, full of expression, he was absorbed in his singing as if intoxicated.

"Thank you, thank you, once more? Okay, okay!" said the young man.

Lai Suo couldn't sit there any longer. Those fashionable, elegant, wealthy young people with nothing to do. His ears filled with laughter and song, and with the sight of their affected gestures, Lai Suo was forced to stand up and hurriedly pay his bill. He pushed the revolving door and stepped out onto broad, straight Ren'ai Road at dusk to once again feel the mysterious life force in the last rays of the sun.

That life force compelled him to take a seat on a bench on the sidewalk across from the towering edifice of the TV station, staring blankly.

"What is it I really want to do?"

At that moment, Lai Suo began to feel a sense of regret. Perhaps he should not have made such a long trip to be there. By this time, his wife had probably cleared the dinner table and was sitting quietly in front of the TV, the children around one side, the middle of the sofa—Lai Suo's seat—empty. He was the head of the family, the father of three children. He sat there with his feet up on the coffee table, laughing at the funny show on TV. His wife and children also laughed. That is a snapshot of the Lai Suo family, their evening fun.

He really shouldn't have made the long trip to be there. He should be sitting in front of the TV, drinking tea and eating soda crackers. Then he would stretch and head off to the bedroom, take off his clothes, climb into bed in the dark, and thus bring the day to a sentimental, good, or indifferent close.

9

It gradually grew dark, and the mercury lamps on both sides of the street went on like a long string of silent firecrackers; the whole street was brightly illuminated in an instant. Lai Suo's eyes followed one bright set of car lights to the next to the end of the street. Time was short! He had to hurry up and think. He focused on the brightly lit TV station. Now, what time did he wish to recall? His childhood or youth, his marriage or his baffling middle age? There were just a few words of resentment for this life of his—"Handing in a blank page." He had disgraced the Lai family. Lai Yun, his older brother, was wealthy; he looked after his brother who had gone to school, arranged his marriage and gave him shares in the factory. The day before Lai Suo's dad passed away, he sadly looked at them and said, "Ah Yun, look after your little brother." Lai Yun was over fifty years old and had a big belly. When he laughed, his eyes narrowed to slits. At that moment, his face was covered with tears and his nose red from crying.

"Dad, you'll get better," said Lai Suo, holding his dad's thick, spotted hand with gray nails in his own. "Next month we'll go to Southeast Asia and look around."

"I'm afraid not," said Lai Suo's dad. "Lai Suo, come here. . . ."

He was partial to his oldest son, while Lai Suo's mom was partial to her younger, more refined son. After Lai Suo was released from prison, he stood cringing in front of his father. His dad looked at him for quite some time, tears streaming down his face; he tried to say something but couldn't utter a word. After a long while, he brought out an old gray suit (it was the suit Ah Yun had tailored for his dad when he was married). "Wear this," he said. "Come along, let's go see your older brother."

"Dad," replied Lai Suo, hesitatingly, "I'd like to go see Mom's grave first."

It wasn't until the first Sunday after he had started working at the jam factory that he finally went to the public cemetery in Muzha. Lai Suo's family, three generations, four adults and four children, were all present. Lai Yun ran around in circles taking care of everything; his wife was tied up with the kids, and Lai Suo's dad stared angrily out the car window without uttering a word. Lai Suo, who was on the verge of tears, kept wringing his hands. There were two cars—one followed the other. The kids kept sticking their hands out the window and shouting, "Grandpa, Grandpa!"

One hour later, they stood at the top of the cemetery, looking down at the desolate graves overgrown with weeds.

"In a few years, they won't be able to squeeze any more in here," commented Lai Suo's dad. He was wrong—seven years later he would be buried in an out-of-the-way little corner, to get to which Lai Suo's family had to climb over grave after grave.

"Ah Suo," said Lai Suo's dad, turning his head, "your mother was thinking of you before she died."

Lai Suo had told himself that he wouldn't cry again. Before the kids had caught up with them, Lai Suo was already bawling as Lai Yun, holding the smallest child, started crying loudly before he could catch his breath.

The caretaker of the cemetery, seeing the situation, said, "Let's burn some spirit money." This put an end to the tears of Lai Suo's family.

"The paint on the inscription has already faded," said Lai Suo, rubbing the gravestone.

. . . OF THE XU FAMILY OF YANSHAN, HENAN PROVINCE. . . .

"Find someone to touch up the inscription and plant some flowers on the grave—what do you say, Dad?" said Lai Yun.

"That won't do," said the caretaker. "Not only will it ruin the *fengshui*, but the goats will come and eat the flowers."

The goats in the area ran wild over the mountain, trampling the graves of Lai Suo's mom and dad as well as urinating and defecating on them.

"That's not right," said Lai Suo, angrily getting up off the bench.

God was a shepherd, or so said the Christians. The neon cross on top of the distant church glowed garishly. Lai Suo walked through the pedestrian underpass. When he came out the other side, he could no longer see that church.

10

Lai Suo arrived at the TV station a half hour before the interview.

Before the guard could do anything, Lai Suo strode through the door with his head held high. The guard gazed at his small, energetic silhouette from behind, wondering where he had seen the guy before.

In this way, Lai Suo had rashly intruded into the labyrinthlike building. It was a modern scientific fusion of dream and reality, art and beauty, along with the fake and the overstated. He went from one studio to the next, from one age to another. He stopped in the Ming dynasty for five minutes, poked his head into the Qing dynasty for a look-see, and at a quarter to eight, entered his own program.

Mr. Han came out of the makeup room wearing a light blue suit, tailor-made to fit, the collar of his Thai silk shirt worn out over his lapels.

His step was firm, his face radiant, and he was in high spirits, as if he were walking to the podium.

"Mr. Han, please take the seat in the middle," said the director, filled with respect. "Our journalists, Zhang and Chen, and Mr. Yang, you will sit over here."

"Are we going to start now?" asked Mr. Han in an extraordinarily calm tone of voice.

"Everyone ready," shouted the director.

Lai Suo stood outside the glass window of the control booth, on the other side of which was a row of monitors displaying the same thing. The control booth operator put on his headphones and crushed out his cigarette. The program was about to start; everyone waited with bated breath. Lai Suo was fascinated by what he saw. He watched as people ran around moving mercury lamps and stage props and testing microphones, and the director made exaggerated gestures.

"Begin," said the director.

"First of all, on behalf of the seventeen million compatriots of our free nation, I would like to welcome Mr. Han on his return to the embrace of the motherland in the anti-Communist camp," said Mr. Yang of the Overseas Chinese Affairs Commission.

"Thank you," said Mr. Han, looking into the camera without blinking. "Allow me to express my heartfelt gratitude for the generosity of the government. In the decades that I was in Japan, there wasn't a moment I didn't feel regret. I apologize to my ancestors and to all my compatriots." At this point he struck the table with his fist. "The Communist Party ruined me."

He had struck the table the same way thirty years before. Lai Suo, who had been sitting in the last row and who was in charge of opening the door, had been awakened by the noise.

"What does the KMT stand for? Tell me." Mr. Han grew increasingly more excited as he spoke. Impassioned, fists flying in the air, he faced the thirty-five members of the Taiwan Democratic Progressive Alliance and shouted himself hoarse. Lai Suo's shocked admiration knew no bounds. A short time before, Mr. Han had warmly asked him about his family, relatives, and friends and their impressions. Lai Suo was too embarrassed to reply—they didn't know, they were illiterate. What about himself? Did he like his job? It wasn't a matter of liking it or not—he did anything Mr. Han asked him to do. That's good. Do you have any problems? No, that's good, that's good. At this point, he turned to ask Mr. Cai, "How's he doing?" Mr. Cai replied in a whisper (Lai Suo could hear him), "Where's this moron from? He actually passed out the flyers at the market, and people used them to wrap meat and fish." "Goodness!" replied Mr. Han, slapping his forehead. "Get someone cut out for the job."

". . . Mr. Han, can you tell us something of your impressions upon first setting foot again on the motherland?"

The cameraman handed the camera to his assistant beside him, pushed open the door, walked over next to Lai Suo, and took a cigarette out of his pocket. He liked interview programs like this one because he didn't have to push the camera all over the place. Music shows, though, he detested on account of the singers who would shake their asses in front of the camera.

"How did you get in? There's no audience allowed for this program." He didn't even glance at Lai Suo.

"The door was open, so I came in."

"The security people must all be asleep," replied the cameraman. "You should go to studio two—it's real lively over there, not boring like this show."

Lai Suo again made no reply—he hadn't come here to answer other people's questions.

"The progress of the motherland is simply unbelievable," said Mr. Han. "I was shocked as soon as I stepped off the plane. I said to myself, This is a modern city! In Japan I had seen reports on TV about the prosperity of Taiwan, but I didn't really believe them."

Lai Suo listened patiently. The cameraman finished his cigarette and said, "God!" and set off toward his assistant.

"You've been to mainland China. What is your impression?"

"I got to know several individuals over there and was duped by them—Sun Qimin and Zhang Wansheng, among others—when they came to Taiwan to fight for unification. If they're not dead, they are still in a labor camp. The authorities in mainland China can suddenly turn hostile and don't consider morality or justice. Our government is different. Although I committed a great wrong"—at this point he paused before continuing—"I was confused at the time. . . ."

Lai Suo had met Sun Qimin and Zhang Wansheng of whom he had spoken; it was a long time ago. They all spoke beautiful Hokkien. In the meeting room at the magazine, Mr. Han had asked everyone to welcome them by standing and applauding. When Sun stood on the podium, he bowed at the waist like a Japanese and said, "Elders and brothers, one and all . . ." He spoke brilliantly and had been specially trained. Initially, Mr. Han had been excited, but the longer he listened, the less interesting he found it. The young Lai Suo noticed that he was on the point of standing up several times but simply shook his head and stayed seated. At that moment, Sun had reached the point—we let the Tibetans, Mongolians, and Miao manage their own affairs. To speak frankly, we don't have the power to govern such a large area, much less this small corner known as Taiwan. Today we would like to help our Taiwan compatriots establish a democratic, progressive, egalitarian, compassionate society. Tens of millions have been eliminated through struggle in mainland China. What has that been all about? It is nothing but a clichéd lie. In a corner of Studio Three, Lai Suo saw through the game of the Communist Party and was very proud of himself.

The Communist Party loves nothing more than peace—Sun paused and took a sip of tea. Mr. Han took the opportunity and leaped up to the podium and said: Everyone, let's have a round of applause. Thank you, Mr. Sun, for your guidance.

"Can you tell us how you discovered the Communist plot?"

"I sensed early on that they wanted to use me to achieve their goal of 'liberating' Taiwan."

Young Mr. Han told them that after Taiwan was liberated, everyone would be given an important position. What about Lai Suo? A county magistrate, perhaps? Which county? It didn't matter which county. Someplace in the north would be best, because each time he went home, everyone would shout, Hey, County Magistrate Lai Suo, hey, Mister County Magistrate!

"It was arranged for many compatriots in Japan to come and see me. I told them of the importance of Taiwan's independence."

"What was their response?"

"At the very beginning, some were interested, but in recent years very few showed any interest. At the time, I asked myself . . ."

At that moment, Lai Suo thought of Fatso Du. Du said disdainfully, "We have Marxism and the KMT has the Three Principles of the People. What about you? What do you have?"

"We have Mr. Han."

"Who is Mr. Han? Who knows him?"

Lai Suo was busy, extremely busy talking with a bunch of people—some were old friends, some were irrelevant people. Even though this was the case, he still had to make time to listen to Mr. Han's speech. The situation was entirely different from that of thirty years before. Lai Suo was using a 1970s mind-set to comment on things that happened in the 1940s. He had the upper hand, the complete advantage. The reporter ought to have turned the camera on him. These young reporters, although in the limelight now, hadn't been born then. Had they seen the Japanese? Had they met a Communist? No. Had they experienced the American bombings? Had they spent time in prison? No. *Goodness. What is it you really want to do? If the camera focused on you, you wouldn't even be able to cut a fart.* Lai Suo listened as the cogs in his brain turned.

"I would like to say one thing more on behalf of all of our compatriots," said Mr. Yang. "I sincerely welcome your return."

"Lastly, Mr. Han, we hope you can say a few words to all those in the world who have been deceived by the Communist Party."

"Okay."

It appeared that the program was about to end. The director gestured, and one of the workmen squatted and touched the electrical cable on the floor. Lai Suo, who was standing at the control booth, planned to step forward to push his way in front of Mr. Han when the program ended.

"So this is where you are," said a young man in a white shirt, blocking his way.

"What are you doing?" asked Lai Suo, annoyed.

"I'm a guard," he said. "You didn't register as a visitor and you're alone. What are you doing here?"

The program had ended a short time before, and Lai Suo was still standing by the steps at the door. Whatever happened, he was waiting for someone.

The automatic doors suddenly opened. A group of people who didn't look at Lai Suo hurried down the steps.

"Mr. Han Zhiyuan," said Lai Suo, blocking the way.

"Yes, what is it?"

"I'm Lai Suo."

"Lai Suo?"

"From *Pan-Asia Magazine*."

"What?"

"The one who sold fruit . . ."

"I don't know you!"

A young man in a pressed suit patted Lai Suo on the shoulder, to help Mr. Han out of his predicament. Then everyone stepped into two black sedans and sped off down the street lit with silver lights.

The immense shadow of the TV station, like some endless nightmare, stretched to the other end of the street. Suddenly there was nothing left in the world save he himself.

"I'm Lai Suo, I'm Lai Suo," he stuttered. "All I wanted to say was that it's been a long time."

11

It was close to midnight when he returned home. He gently opened the door, turned on the light, and placed a few things he had picked up in Taipei on the sofa—sleepwear for his wife, coloring books for the kids, and a box of chocolates.

At that moment, the Holland clock on the wall chimed several times, the hour and minute hands standing straight up. It was an end and a beginning, a starting point and a finale.

Without moving, Lai Suo slowly raised his head.

Translated by John Balcom

the intelligent man

Several days after the Republic of China and the United States broke off relations, Yang T'ai-sheng began to consider carefully his own future and that of Taiwan. Never in his entire life had he made such a big decision, not even the day he decided to marry Chu Yu-hsiang—it had only taken a few minutes to weigh the sacred duties of marriage and the high cost of living and other such things.

But reality is not like three buses arriving simultaneously; one could board any one of them without consideration, and even if a mistake were made, one could always return to the point of departure. Reality is not a bus, but the road leading to a goal. Therefore, Yang T'ai-sheng seriously inquired among his many friends, all of whom, in turn, responded earnestly: "In times like these, if at all possible, go to America, because in America you can find many unexpected opportunities."

He then quickly sold off all assets at hand, which included some stocks, a house, and a used Ford (the funny thing was that the buyer was one of those friends who had advised him to go to America). All the money was sent to America through a relative in the import-export business. It was exciting to change NTD into dollars. However, when the airplane was high above the Pacific Ocean, Yang T'ai-sheng suddenly felt sad. Then, just like MacArthur on the day he left the Philippines, he said to himself, "I shall return."

At first, Yang T'ai-sheng took his wife and daughter to stay at his sister's home in New York. His brother-in-law owned a Cantonese dim sum tea house there. In America, if the basement of a house is well ventilated, it can be turned into nice living quarters with just a little imagination and some enthusiasm, because America is a place full of possibilities.

To work as a waiter in a dim sum tea house takes a minimum of training and a little psychological readjustment. The most difficult part is learning to speak English. But in just three months, Yang T'ai-sheng, a college graduate in history, learned to speak English much better than the elderly Chinese who had lived there for thirty years.

As the situation in Taiwan cleared up, Yang T'ai-sheng slowly came to realize that it made no sense for him to have come all the way from Taiwan to America to work as a waiter. So, on Double Ten, when the streets of Chinatown were filled with the lively sounds of gongs and drums, Yang T'ai-sheng discussed the matter with his brother-in-law, who told him that indeed the grass is greener in America, but one has to watch for the opportunities. His sister and brother-in-law wished him good luck.

Thus a new family was born in Monterey Park.

Like other Chinese who had come to America from Taiwan to find "a turning point in life," he felt the first step was to buy a house. So Yang T'ai-sheng, through a friend of his brother-in-law's, boldly put down 70 percent of his working capital and bought a house, which, 10 years later, he told everyone he had obtained at a real bargain. The house was situated on a big lot. Six years later he built another house on it, which he rented out to a guy who owned a travel agency.

He had a house and he was very ambitious, but what kind of business should he get into?

Since Peter Wang had officially announced his candidacy for congressman, everyone, especially the people flowing in from Taiwan, speculated that Monterey Park would develop fast in the near future.

Yang T'ai-sheng, with foresight, looked around and discovered that many people didn't know how to decorate their American-style homes. Some people even had sealed up the fireplaces in their living rooms, because they thought that a fireplace was used only for cooking. He decided to open a furniture store so that the poor immigrants from Taiwan could live a really American life.

Five years later, an old woman told him that she couldn't stand the overstuffed American sofas and that she missed the old-style rocking chairs from home. Out of sympathy—and with a keen eye for business—Yang T'ai-sheng imported five of the rocking chairs. Unexpectedly, the chairs sold out within a week. T'ai-yuan Furniture Shop saw the advent of a new age as Yang T'ai-sheng began importing furniture from Taiwan. Soon, there were no longer any pieces of furniture made in the U.S.A. to be found in the shop. His sister's whole family came from far away to congratulate him. He proudly told them, "I just can't forget my origins."

After this he regularly went back to Taiwan twice each year.

In 1981, NBC ran a six-day television program, *A Trip to Taiwan*, that made all the Chinese who were from Taiwan and now living in Monterey Park homesick. Many people told him that they missed their lives in the countryside of Taiwan.

Two times a year, he went back to Taiwan to purchase the kind of furniture that would cure their nostalgia. The second time he went to Taiwan in 1981, he was out in the countryside when he was struck by an inspiration. Due to this inspiration, combined with the Taiwan policy of "Steady Growth," he boldly made the second important decision of his lifetime. T'ai-yuan entered a stage of multinational enterprise: next to the Fu-ho Bridge in Yung-ho, Yang T'ai-sheng opened the Antique Furniture Assembly Factory.

The workers at the shop had the ability to put together old wooden furniture purchased in the countryside and, like plastic surgeons, give it a second life.

All together he had five people working for him and an accountant, a young lady. To give them more incentive in their work, he told them, "As soon as the business gets off the ground, you will have the opportunity to go to America, where . . ." It sounded reasonable.

The young accountant, Yeh Mei-chu, was pretty and competent. One night in November, after sending out an order of merchandise worth US $100,000, the two of them drank some wine. Stimulated in part by the excitement of their work and in part by the desire he had already conceived for Yeh Mei-chu, Yang T'ai-sheng later told his wife that he had done this for a serious reason—he wanted a son. His wife, though disagreeing with his idea, did compromise, on the condition that "she was not to be allowed to set foot in America."

Thus the problem was solved. Each time Yang T'ai-sheng returned to Taiwan, he made a strenuous effort to produce a son. He also picked out a name for the baby in advance: Nien-t'ai. But Nien-t'ai never came. Yang T'ai-sheng, aside from making more concerted efforts, attempted to persuade Yeh Mei-chu to go to the hospital for a checkup. Yeh Mei-chu refused to go. "Your sperm count must be too low. They say that people who fly too often will have this sort of trouble. I got some Chinese herbal medicine for you. They say . . ."

In the spring of 1985, the Taiwan Strait was calm and tranquil. However, the furniture market in Monterey Park was in a state of turbulence. A man named Qin, who had immigrated from mainland China, had imported Ming dynasty furniture, causing a small but economically profitable "search for roots."

"Damn," Yang T'ai-sheng complained to his wife. "What kind of nonsense is all this to-do about the Ming dynasty things?" It didn't matter what he said. After Qin imported a chamber pot once used by a eunuch and caused a surge in sales, Yang T'ai-sheng declared he had given up two of his principles: no trading relations with or visiting relatives in mainland China. (Relatives in mainland China were always writing to ask for money, and his wife had already visited China twice.)

"I guess I'd better make a trip to the other side." With a Taiwan passport, the best way to enter mainland China was through Hong Kong. Before his departure, his wife contacted the relatives over there. As soon as they heard of his coming, they planned a big welcome party for him.

Thus Yang T'ai-sheng was easily able to open a factory in the Xiamen Special Economic Zone. All together he had eleven people working for him. "As soon as business gets off the ground, you will have the opportunity to go to Taiwan, where . . ."

During his second inspection trip, his relatives recommended a young lady from Shanghai to be his administrative assistant. The young lady, a graduate of the English department of Fudan University, was pretty and competent. The moment he laid eyes on her, he felt he could transfer his "Taiwan experience" to her. From her desire to look pretty, Yang T'ai-sheng understood that she possessed a high degree of "bourgeois liberality." So, one night in the autumn of 1986 when the streets were filled with the lively sounds of drums and gongs celebrating the anniversary of the success of the revolution, and after he had loaned her family a sum of money to repair their house, he "united" with her.

Pan Jia, his mainland mistress, was a shy but brave little woman. Ever since she was a little girl, she' knew how to fight for her rights. She also realized that giving Yang T'ai-sheng a son was the basis of all duty and power. From October to December, the two of them struggled unceasingly for a "new generation."

On Christmas Eve, Yang T'ai-sheng returned to Taiwan. Mei-chu treated him coldly, because she had just talked on the phone with his wife in America. "You can't wrap fire in paper. Knowledge of your affairs has spread all over the States. Your first wife just called and told me that a relative in mainland China told her that you've got a Shanghai woman."

"That's not so." Inwardly he cursed this age of global communication networks.

"Pan Jia," she said, starting to cry, "that communist bitch."

"She's not a communist," said Yang T'ai-sheng as he dodged a vase thrown in his direction. "Don't throw that one, it's crystal and is worth $400."

"Then you're going to stick up for her! She plans to come and share our property."

"I must have a son to carry on the Yang family name."

"Communist bitch!"

"She is very capable, and can take care of our interests on the mainland," pleaded Yang T'ai-sheng. "Besides, she's definitely no communist."

A Christmas song came on the TV. It was sung in English and was filled with a sense of peace and tranquility. Yang T'ai-sheng recognized the singer as Bing Crosby, whose old records continued to sell by the hundreds of thousands every year.

Mei-chu thought of his first wife in America, who had just called her. It almost seemed that the two of them stood on the same side; this made her feel a little better. "No matter what you say, or under whatever circumstances, that Shanghai woman should not be allowed to set foot in Taiwan."

Thus resolved, the "cold war" began. Yang T'ai-sheng spent the entire month he was in Taiwan thinking about how to solve this sticky problem. Finally, with a heavy heart, he carried these problems with him as he uneasily returned to Monterey Park. During the two weeks before New Year's Day, his wife didn't give him a single day of peace. In various ways, she reminded him that he was a big fool. "The one in Taiwan is understandable," she said, sneering at him. "But that one in mainland China could be your daughter." His daughter, who was then studying at Harvard University, had called to inform him that she couldn't make it home to celebrate Chinese New Year. That was it! For the first time in his life, Yang T'ai-sheng felt deeply distressed. "You know, my old lady-killer, the hair on the back of your head is beginning to turn white. Here, let me pull some out for you to look at."

"I remember the lively New Year's festivities of the past." The couple sat facing each other across a long table.

"You probably miss your homes in Taiwan and Xiamen, don't you?"

His greatest desire in life was to unify his family. In the summer of 1987, the first "family conference" was convened in Singapore.

Why had Singapore been chosen? Because each of the wives had sworn that the others were not allowed to enter her territory. Naturally he had considered Hong Kong, but it was too close to mainland China. Choosing Hong Kong might have given the mistaken impression that he favored one of them over the others. Besides, he had an old friend in Singapore who could arrange everything; on top of which, Singapore was clean and quiet, just the place for anyone who wanted to sit down and talk calmly.

The Royal Hotel, located in the middle of downtown, was a thirty-story building. From the windows one could look over the edifices of the finely planned "third China."

The rooms had been prepared. The largest room had a small conference room attached to it. Yang T'ai-sheng and his first wife stayed in that room, on the twenty-second floor. The second wife was on the twenty-first floor and the third wife was on the twentieth floor. It had been arranged this way to prevent them from running into each other in the hallway.

After everyone had lunched in their own room and rested, it came time for the meeting. The first wife was dressed in a light voile dress from Dior's branch shop in Los Angeles. The second was wearing a Western-style dress, hand tailored by Lancaster designers in Taipei, and the third wore a black *qiipao*, the masterpiece of a famous Shanghai dressmaker. The four of them sat around a round table. Yang T'ai-sheng looked to his right and to his left, feeling like an emperor of old. His three wives glanced at one another from the corners of their eyes.

After a moment, Yang T'ai-sheng cleared his throat and said, "This is a historical moment. We thank the past generations of our ancestors for this blessing." His inspiration welled up like a spring, as if he were once again a college student indulging in loud and empty talk. "That the entire family can be together to discuss and plan our future is a significant breakthrough for the nation." As he said this he cursed himself inwardly; he also heard his first wife snort, but pretended not to hear. "Of course, there are some technical problems that must be resolved," he continued. "For example, every Chinese New Year we should all get together. . . ."

"Don't forget the conditions you have already agreed to. I don't want the neighbors laughing at me!" said the first wife, unable to hold back any longer.

"I can't have you coming to my place, I still have a position in society," said the second.

The third lowered her voice as if she had been wronged. "Where I come from, committing adultery must be reformed through labor."

"Nonsense, there is no reform through labor over there anymore." Yang T'ai-sheng stood up, waving his hands to silence them. "Commit, hell, nobody can even visit." Then he sat down in a fury, tapping the table with his fingers. The three wives started talking to one another about their dresses. After a while they changed the subject to prices, as if they wanted to leave Yang T'ai-sheng out in the cold.

Yang T'ai-sheng looked around. Suddenly he was puzzled, because he didn't know how to arrange things for that night. He couldn't help scratching his head, thinking about these three women who urgently needed his most productive energies to live together.

"That's enough!" shouted Yang T'ai-sheng. The three of them became silent. In a moment, he recovered his authority. "We will continue this meeting tomorrow."

There was still no progress the next day, but his three wives were becoming more intimate with one another and seemed to have arrived at some sort of tacit understanding. A week later, the first wife made the first move by declaring that the three of them had reached an agreement. Under this agreement, Hong Kong was the site chosen for producing an heir. The entire family would stay in Hong Kong for one year, during which time every one of them had to do their best to produce a son for the Yang family. If one got pregnant, the whole family would live in the lucky mother's territory. If nothing happened, they would split up, living separately as they had done before. The suggestions were pretty good, and Yang T'ai-sheng laughingly accepted.

After the agreement was reached, they spent a week sightseeing. Singapore was indeed a pleasant place, full of potential. With great business acumen, Yang T'ai-sheng couldn't help checking it out.

The day before their tour was to end, Yang T'ai-sheng announced to his three wives, "While you were shopping, I took the opportunity to look around and analyze the business situation here. I also talked on the phone with a number of friends"—he paused and looked around at his wives—"and they all agreed with my point of view, that it is possible for me to open a branch office here."

Translated by Yingtsih Balcom

how to measure
the width of a ditch

1

No matter what you say, measuring the width of a ditch will never be an interesting topic of conversation. When we regale our friends with words, we most frequently resort to topics such as male-female relations, economics, scandals, movies, and jokes.

We mull over witticisms, lick our humorous lips, and then tighten our vocal cords to emit sounds in all wavelengths. If these sounds are organized, possess meaning, or are interesting, we then dub them topics of conversation.

Yes, I too have significant means at my disposal to deal with these superficial topics. In addition to the few mentioned previously, I can also converse about the weather, medicine, and shells (of which I have collected a whole drawer full).

I wouldn't exactly say that hearing me talk is enjoyable, but neither is it a torture, unless, that is, I am incautious and let slip the matter of measuring the width of a ditch. When that happens, normally the facial muscles of the person listening suddenly contract, the lines around his or her mouth deepen, and their eyes grow larger, forming an enigmatic expression that possesses a strong satirical power, the sight of which immediately cuts me short.

Let me say something about the title of this piece—"How to Measure the Width of a Ditch." With regard to this issue, most people would accept a counterquestion in reply: How do you measure the width of the soul?

This form of question and answer is frequently encountered in academic debates on metaphysics. For example:

"Where is God?"

"Where is man?"

Or in the *koans* of Chan Buddhism:

"Master, please give me a dharma-door with which to quiet my mind."

"Show me your mind and I'll quiet it for you."

Thus, when wit is used carelessly, it can easily sink to the level of profanity. I must avoid this at all costs. What's more, the soul and a ditch cannot be discussed in the same breath, though a certain connection does exist between them. Let it be said, though, that this connection is the main reason for my tossing and turning at night.

How do you measure the width of a ditch? How do you measure the width of the soul? Why I am I so fond of this question? Why can't I rid myself of the habit of thinking about measuring the width of a ditch at any time and in any place?

This city is covered with a network of different kinds of ditches: irrigation ditches, drainage ditches, sewers, and even the perpetually smelly old-style sewers.

I asked the Public Works Department how many ditches are there in the city, but they couldn't tell me.

"Why don't you go ask the Environmental Protection Department?"

I called four times before a young woman finally answered the phone and politely asked me, "Sir, may I ask why you want to know how many ditches there are?"

I told her that it was a matter about which someone had to be concerned.

Ditches serve as the city's excrement channel, just like our assholes. It's not something people like to discuss, but someone has to be concerned about it. All the more so since they're so quickly disappearing from sight, like earthworms burrowing underground, breathing underfoot, moaning, writhing; if at all possible, they'd hiccup and the stench would come pouring out through the grated cover.

However, even this kind of grated cover allows you a peep into the world underground, though they are gradually being replaced by airtight concrete; they are capable of supporting a truck and an elephant weighing several tons and give the road's surface a classier look, making them the unsung heroes who protect the appearance of the city. So, in short, someone must step forward and be concerned about this matter.

"What matter? Which one?"

"Listen. The first question is: How many ditches are there in this city? The second question is: What method do you use to measure their widths?"

"I'm not certain about the answer to your first question. As to your second question, my guess is that they use a tape measure. It must be, because I have seen the water main repairman—"

"Miss," I replied, interrupting her, "you have totally misunderstood my question. I said 'ditch' and not 'water main.'"

I then repeated my concerns about the disappearance of ditches and how no one really cared.

But regardless of my efforts, I couldn't make the young lady on the other end of the line understand. She simply muttered a few apologies.

"I should be the one to apologize," I said as I hung up. "When I have the answer, I'll let you know."

Then it came to me that if I didn't start from the beginning, no one would understand this matter, much less its importance.

2

On May 30, 1960, we decided to measure the width of a ditch.

There were five of us.

I was born in 1949. In 1971, I graduated from the university with a degree in physics, and in 1976, I began working at Rainbow Peanut Butter Company, where I have worked to this day. Many people have asked me, why peanut butter and not a peanut sauce for satay? They say that the long-term prospects for satay sauce look good, and are related to the taste for eating hot pot in the winter, among other factors. My reply is that as a young person I read and was deeply touched by a piece written by the author Xu Dishan titled "The Peanut" in which he says, "One should study the peanut to learn how to conduct oneself."

In the '80s, the boss decided that peanut butter was no longer enough for him, so he decided to invest in shoe manufacturing.

A year later, Rainbow Company was already producing pigskin soccer shoes and had even signed a contract to provide one soccer team with their shoes free of charge for a year. The boss also hoped that I would sell shoes for him. There was no way I could refuse. So, from manager of the peanut butter production department I was transferred to the post of assistant manager of the athletic shoe business. The gap between the two was huge and would be the equivalent of an author like Xu Dishan, who eulogized the peanut, becoming an insurance salesman.

That very same year, I began writing poetry, which I did for a while before switching to science fiction.

My first work appeared in the literary supplement of an evening paper. It was a story about an alien with eight clawed limbs wearing shoes. Because it had eight clawed limbs, putting on shoes was a complicated thing.

Unfortunately, the story didn't receive much notice. Actually, the idea behind the story came entirely from my boss. One day he sighed and uttered the following words: "Why do people only have two feet? Why not four? Or six?"

In a word, I fervently wanted to become a respected science fiction writer, but to this date, I have only finished three pieces.

Lai Xiaosheng and I are the same age. In 1975, he sent me a postcard out of the blue from someplace down south. I don't know what has become of him since then.

Zeng Yiping. My memories of him are somewhat vague. I seem to recall that he was the tallest of us and always brought up the rear.

Lu Fang died in a traffic accident in 1976. I clipped the story from the newspaper and stuck it in the autograph album for our grade-school reunion. It was a major accident. The bus he was on was broadsided by a train at a railway crossing. The pieces of broken metal from the shattered body of the bus became sharp deadly weapons. Six bodies lay scattered piecemeal for a distance of a hundred meters on both sides of the tracks.

Chen Jinde is the only grade-school classmate with whom I'm still in touch. One evening after I transferred to the athletic shoe department in 1981, I had a brainstorm. I opened the phone book and found that there were eight people listed with the same name. Ever so patiently, I began dialing each one until I located him.

"Do you recall the name Xie Mingmin?"

"Xie Mingmin?"

"Twenty-one years ago. Section four, sixth grade at Qingping Elementary School."

Silence. I saw that there were two more Chen Jindes left in the phone book and was about to give up.

"Ah, is that . . . is that really you?"

We arranged to meet the following day.

I located him at the Western-style restaurant by having him paged. We didn't hesitate in the slightest to thrust our hands forward to shake. His palm was pudgy and moist like an orange.

"Wow!" He gave my hand a frightful shaking. "I never thought, I never thought . . ."

We both ordered two complete KFC meals. The steaming hot fried chicken smelled so good. The golden oil ran down Chen Jinde's chin, which he wiped with great brio with his paper napkin.

"How did you know that I like to eat this?"

"Have you forgotten? Coming here was your idea," I said, laughing.

"What about the others? Were you able to contact them all? Why don't we form a students' association and get together once or twice a year?"

"Lai Xiaosheng moved to the south; I'm not sure about Zeng Yiping—he may have left the country. Lu Fang died in a traffic accident several years ago. What about you? What have you been up to?"

Chen Jinde told me that after finishing primary school, he studied for two years in a junior high before goofing off. He worked as an unskilled laborer, doing legwork for a medicinal plaster salesman and an insurance salesman, and was now selling used cars and auto parts.

"And you? You look like you've done well. What do you do? Own a barbershop?"

"I work in an athletic shoe factory."

"Adidas or Puma?"

"Rainbow. It's pretty famous. We have commercials on TV every Monday, Wednesday, and Friday. I'm sure you've seen them. First you see a rainbow, and then our shoes walk from one end to the other. It's pretty interesting. I'm sure you've seen it."

Chen Jinde didn't recall seeing the commercial. He scratched his head, rolled his eyes, and then with a wave of his hand, changed the subject. "I seem to recall that big ditch you mentioned yesterday. But what is it we wanted to do by that stinking ditch?"

"We all wanted," I began, shifting position, "to measure the width of the ditch."

3

We planned to measure the width of the ditch on May 30, 1960.

But as detective fiction author Lin Deng said, "Before the tale actually took place, it had been developing in secret for a long time."

For this reason, I must begin on the morning of that day so as to let everyone know the motive for measuring the width of the ditch.

The weather on the morning of May 30 ought to have been clear.

"Give me fifty cents!"

"For what?" my dad asked. "Didn't I just give you fifty cents yesterday?"

"To buy a notebook." It was an old ploy. I already had one in which I had written on only two pages. All I had to do was tear out the two pages.

My dad was a nice person who liked a drink and to play the *huqin*, but never at the same time. He passed away a long time ago. I still have his photos, in each of which he is seen smiling as if he knew that one day his son would describe his smile in a work of fiction. I don't know why I have always felt that I owe him something.

(If any of my readers are interested in him, you can write to the following address: Literary Supplement of the *United Daily News*, 555 Section 4 Zhongxiao East Road, Taipei. [I'm preparing to submit this piece to them.])

In high spirits, I then took the money to school.

By the end of the third period class, I had already used thirty cents. My last dime I gave to a girl student by the name of Goldfish, who was perhaps the poorest student on campus. I gave her a dime and she let me stick my hand up her skirt, which was made from old flour sacks.

Many years later, I told this to my girlfriend, with whom I was living at the time (of course I was not the protagonist of my tale). She was furious and said I had made up the story purely influenced by the gossip pages.

"You've read too many salacious and violent stories."

"I'm not kidding," I said. "The girl is now a television newscaster."

"Nonsense!"

(We had a huge fight over this. Three months later, she left me. Before she left, she said, "Megalomaniac!" At first I was never going to forgive her for as long as I lived, but the moment I wrote this, I suddenly forgave her. From this one can see the cathartic power of fiction, especially for authors.)

Anyway, my pockets were as empty as ever. Lu Fang proposed going to the edge of the big ditch after school, so I joined them.

The five of us set off from the side gate of the school. The shortest of the bunch, I walked in the middle while Zeng Yiping brought up the rear. Lai Xiaosheng was at the head—he always saw himself as our leader.

"Heads up, everyone!" Lai Xiaosheng shouted. "Up ahead is the virgin forest."

The so-called virgin forest was nothing but a bunch of bushes. Lai Xiaosheng brandished a stick symbolically.

"We don't want to go there," said Zeng Yiping behind me.

"If we don't go there, we can go home and do our homework," I said.

At this point, Chen Jinde chimed in with some bad words about our teachers.

However, strange at it may seem, twenty-one years later in the KFC restaurant, Chen Jinde spoke in an entirely different fashion.

"I remember teacher Wang Wuxiong. He showed a great deal of concern for me and hoped that I would test into a decent junior high, but my family's financial situation wasn't so good. . . . "

"The day we founded the Ditch Gang, you told me that teacher Wang despised you more than anyone because he often threw chalk at your head."

"That's impossible—teacher Wang liked me more than anyone else."

"Okay! Then you should at least remember that other event."

"I have no recollection of it," said Chen Jinde. "I don't recall that we ever organized a gang with such a strange name."

(Chen Jinde, no doubt, is a troublemaker, whether in real life or fiction.)

Let me go back and talk about the circumstances when we left school that day. Our group of explorers left through the side gate and went down a narrow path through entwined bushes, trees, and a bamboo fence.

I saw the path again in 1983 (the year I was called up for military service) and again in 1985 (after completing my service) and again in 1987. Since then, I have spent a couple of afternoons a year walking around the area.

It was probably between 1985 and 1987 when the bushes were dug out to make room for a cobblestone road that motorcycles could use. Nonconforming buildings made of steel and wood were erected on either side. In 1989, the nonconforming buildings were torn down, the road widened, and long. narrow, three-story residential buildings erected on either side. It was at that time that the ditch was moved underground.

Four years later, I bought a Ford and that very day went to see the old neighborhood. I slowed down and circled the school.

The school looked small and cramped. Then I went down the small path, or, I should say, the avenue, a four-lane street with seven- and eight-story buildings on either side. In a matter of minutes, I arrived at the former site of the big ditch.

I stopped my car, planning to relive some childhood events there above the ditch. Unexpectedly, a horn sounded behind me. That sound is one of humiliation in the big city, but all the more so in the suburbs. I finally parked my car thirty meters away in front of a coffee house. I spent the entire afternoon inside, staring blankly out the window.

The five of us continued on, leaping and shouting as we went, as if we wanted to let everyone know how happy we were.

After a while, we stifled our laughter and breathed deeply through our noses because the foul odor of burning trash filled the air.

A while later, we smelled chicken manure (perhaps it was dog shit— it's hard to be certain after the passage of so many years). After that stink, light and shadow flickered before our eyes. It was a small dirt mound in which were embedded pieces of broken glass, slag, and chunks of brick. We carefully climbed to the top of the mound of dirt and stood in the bright light and the breeze, which smelled of dry grass, and looked down at the big ditch snaking away at our feet.

4

When I thought about giving a complete picture of the big ditch, an idea suddenly came to me: Why not draw a picture of it?

So I put down what I was doing and ran to the stationery store, where I purchased a box of colored pens and a sheet of paper.

(The previous lines were written upon my return from the stationery store. If a reader should ask why I chose a box of colored pens and not crayons or pencils, my reply would be that the stationery store sold only colored pens or that upon entering the store all I saw were colored pens. They cost eighteen *yuan*.)

I will now begin to draw!

Note: the ratio of this picture is approximately 100–150:1. But, dear Reader, please don't take out a ruler to measure the width of the ditch in this picture and then multiply that figure by 150. In doing so, it would be you, not the author, me, measuring the ditch. As to the color, there will be some difference from reality. And if the editor rejects my suggestion, the picture will be in black and white and the ditch will be gray. It will be the same as the color of the river you saw recently. But the color of river water was different in those days, as was that of the ditch water. At this

point, I'd like to remind everyone: do not let Chang E laugh at our dirty river water.

5

I was quite satisfied with the results and felt it could help explain the matter of how to measure the width of a ditch. So I inserted the picture in an envelope in preparation for finding someone on whom its usefulness could be tested.

At this point in the story, many readers might feel impatient. If that is the case, I have a number of suggestions:

1. You can immediately stop reading and think of a way to forget what you have read.

2. You must be anxious to learn how the author measured the width of the ditch. If that is the case, I will tell you. At the time we carried a bow and arrows. We tied a string to the end of the arrow and shot the arrow into the bark of a tree on the opposite side of the ditch. Then we pulled the arrow back and measured the length of the string, and we had our answer.

3. If you are dissatisfied with the above two suggestions, I'll make another. For the moment don't think about how to measure the width of a ditch and patiently keep on reading.

I gave the young lady at the Environmental Protection Department another call.

"I called a few days ago and asked how many ditches there are. Do you remember?"

"Ah!" she cried out softly.

"My name is Xie."

"I didn't expect you to call again, Mr. Xie."

"Why not?"

"People always call me." She continued, "May I ask why you are so interested in that question?"

I detected a sound. I guessed that it was the sound of someone covering their mouth to laugh.

"A lot of people ask the same question, but for the moment I can't explain it." I said, "How about this. Are you busy? I'll buy you a cup of coffee."

"I don't go out with strangers."

"I'm no stranger. I told you who I am." I had told her my profession and age. "Besides, I can meet you at your office. Public offices such as yours have someone responsible for answering people's questions, right? In this way, I'm just trying to adopt a more informal approach."

"Can I bring a colleague?"

Pouring out your heart to someone uninvolved is risky, but also exciting.

Thus I carried a copy of the *United Daily News* (this was our prearranged signal). I waited at the coffee house for five minutes before two young ladies appeared.

"Mr. Xie, this is my colleague Miss Ma." I asked them to have a seat. Miss Ma, who was wearing glasses, was tittering.

"It's very funny, isn't it?" I asked.

"No need to ask." Miss Chen laughed as well. "Miss Ma and I work in the same office. I told her about the matter you mentioned."

I laughed too. Laughing, I sighed to myself as I sized up the two young ladies, their mediocre looks and their childish makeup.

"You must both be curious, right?"

"Yes!" said Miss Chen. "I receive several strange phone calls every day, but yours is the strangest of all."

"It's so interesting!" commented Miss Ma.

"What kind of strange calls?" I asked.

"One guy called and said there was a snake burrow in his rooftop garden. I told him to call 911."

"How interesting!" said Miss Ma.

I figured the next thing she was going to say was "How amusing!"

"Don't think for a moment that I'm joking. If an atomic bomb were to explode, just think of how many people could take shelter in the underground ditches. If an atomic bomb went off, everything on the streets would be incinerated. The only thing on your mind then would be to flee into an underground ditch, shouting as you did so, 'Look at this ditch— why didn't the city government make it larger?'"

"How frightening," said Miss Ma, adding her two cents.

I stared at her as I continued, "That's why I have developed the habit of measuring ditches. Whenever I pass a ditch, whether it is concealed underground or in the open, I can't help but ask myself, 'How wide is it really? How many people will fit into it?' That's why I called to ask how many ditches there are in the city and what method you use to measure them."

"So Mr. Xie is an atomic bomb-phobe," said Miss Chen.

"How amusing," said Miss Ma.

As could be expected, the outcome was that Miss Ma consented to help me find an answer to my above-mentioned query as well as hinting at the possibility of further developing a friendship. I, however, actually felt depressed, extremely depressed. Good Lord! What had happened? What was wrong? Originally I had brought along my picture to help explain, but I had made a simple matter overly complicated, even deviating from my main purpose. It was the same as when I wrote that sci-fi story titled "The Eight-Limbed Alien." On account of a few technical errors, neither readers nor author could tell which was hand and which was foot.

Well, what eventually happened to those two young ladies? I'm sure a number of readers will be interested in learning if I became friends with one of them or if we fell in love.

I won't say yes and I won't say no.

My answer is that the future developments with the two young ladies have nothing to do with this story. They returned to their real lives. Like you, as far as they were concerned, this matter was simply one of those occasional variables in life.

As you read this story, you also are "involved in" the story; it's just that the way you enter the story is completely different from the way those two young ladies entered.

The difference is that "you" are not a specific, well-defined object. But if you read this story in the morning paper one day, and before finishing the piece, you contact me at once, then in that case you might really set foot in my story.

But given the present circumstances, this might be hard to achieve in terms of technique, unless, that is, the way literary supplements do things changes completely. (For example, a short story appears in its entirety in one month, publishing just once a week, or you change your conception of the integrity of a work of fiction.)

For this reason, the two young ladies must exit the stage. They nearly dragged me off track. So I called and told them that the matter of measuring the width of a ditch had been nothing but a big joke.

6

Allow me to record the following passage:

We understand the outer world through our senses. When we perceive some phenomena, we sometimes endow certain of them with special significance as a result of how our senses function and how our brain processes stimuli. There is an extremely important feature to this process: we fragment the gestalt of the time-space continuum surrounding us and for this reason perceive our environment as being composed of distinct categories of objects as well as breaking the flow of time into a series of discrete units.

After going through the unexpected twists and turns between fiction and reality, we feel a bit more courageous and intelligent when it comes to facing the actual events that occurred on May 30, 1960.

The Truth

May 30, 1960.

By the time we reached the big ditch, there were only four of us left. (Chen Jinde had returned home at the last minute.)

Lai Xiaosheng, Zeng Yiping, Lu Fang, and I.

The four of us lay facedown on the concrete bank of the ditch, looking down at the reflections in the water. Actually the sky was very clear, and the water flowed clear, making the surface a mirror.

"I can see the future," I said to my friends.

"Then tell us our fates," said Lai Xiaosheng.

"Lai Xiaosheng, you will mail me a postcard in 1975," I said. "Zeng Yiping, you and I will lose contact."

"And me?" asked Lu Fang.

"I don't want to say."

"Tell us, tell us, tell us."

"You guys are forcing me—I won't be responsible for the consequences."

"Tell us."

"Lu Fang, you will die in a traffic accident in 1976."

"What nonsense!"

"What about you?" asked Zeng Yiping.

"In 1985, I will write a piece titled 'How to Measure the Width of a Ditch.'"

"What! You're saying that you are going to measure the width of a ditch in the future?" asked Zeng Yiping.

"Right!"

"Why don't we try now? There's no need to wait that long," said Lai Xiaosheng.

"Okay, but how do you propose to do it?"

The four of us sat beside the ditch, devoting a good deal of gray matter to the problem. Night found us still there, unable to figure out a way to accomplish it.

Translated by John Balcom

zero

Yes, we are about to make history. We—you and I—the members of the committee, now find ourselves at a turning point in history. Beyond this point lies what our ancestors extolled—that transcendent and sacred Golden Age, perfect in every way.

Yes, members of the committee, we shall never forget the last century, a benighted century shrouded in darkness and destruction, a century in which human beings dragged out their animal-like existences, a century that our textbooks refer to as the "Dark Ages."

I believe that at this moment, all of you, like me, are taking part in this committee meeting with profound gratitude and humility. This meeting is unlike all previous annual meetings in that everything we say, every word we speak, shall be recorded in the annals of history so that posterity might savor our accomplishments and discuss the great success of this meeting with relish. Like the number zero, it marks an end as well as a beginning.

Allow me to express my gratitude to Nanning and to Mr. Max Kristen, as well as the committee members, who, over the years, through their contributions, have provided the perfect environment in which to begin this unprecedented plan that will allow humanity to advance to the highest stage of evolution in the universe as well as attain and enjoy the supreme happiness bestowed by Nanning.

CHAIRMAN OF THE SECOND NANNING COMMITTEE

1

After emptying the last canister of growth formula into his field, Xi Jin patted his hands and prepared to knock off after a day's work.

At that moment a strange occurrence on the northern horizon attracted his attention. He looked up, fixed his gaze on the horizon line, and watched the gradual appearance of several silver flying objects. The small, saucer-shaped objects glowed and seemed to appear and disappear amid the evening clouds filling the sky. Xi Jin concentrated his gaze for a while. How he wished he could ride in one of those saucers, even if just for a minute. But he was a farmer, and according to the professional caste classification, he belonged to the irreplaceable forty-fifth level. Short of a miracle, he was destined to be a farmer his entire life.

Considering this, Xi Jin couldn't help but sigh. The strange occurrence on the horizon had vanished—no doubt the flying machines had penetrated the ozone layer and were headed for some destination in the vast universe. It was nearly dark. Xi Jin turned on the farm's sunlamps. Brilliant green plants appeared immediately before him. He set off in the direction of his house.

Strangely, there was no one at home. Xi Jin turned on all the lights. Where could she have gone? He paced and thought. Where could his wife be if she were not in the kitchen getting dinner? He sat down on the living room sofa, lit a cigarette, and stared blankly at the television screen on the wall.

"Xi Jin! Xi Jin!" He opened his eyes at the sound of a woman's voice.

"Oh, you're back," said Xi Jin. "I must have dozed off."

"You'll never guess where I've been, never."

She was an ordinary-looking middle-aged woman with a pair of warm, dark eyes. Her thin face was red with excitement.

"Let me guess, you went to the commissary to buy something?"

"Wrong, wrong."

"Then you must have gone to Yidong's place to play video games."

"Wrong again. I'll tell you. I went to the Ministry of Domestic Affairs."

"Ministry of Domestic Affairs! What were you doing there?"

"Listen to me, Xi Jin. What is it that you have wanted more than anything else in life?"

Xi Jin sat up straight and looked at his wife next to him as she tried to control her excitement. They had lived together for twenty years, but she had never been able to open that secret compartment deep in his heart. At that moment, a silver flying saucer filled his mind; there it was, free from all constraints, performing all sorts of maneuvers—rising, diving, looping, rolling. . . .

"What have I wanted more than anything else?"

"A child," shouted his wife, unable to control herself any longer. "Xi Jin, we're going to have a child of our own, a precious, cute, lively, bouncing baby."

"Good lord, what are you saying?"

"This afternoon I received notification from the Ministry of Domestic Affairs," she said, out of breath. "They told me that the application for a child we've made for the last twenty years had finally been granted. Think about it—we've waited twenty years for a child of our own."

2

A year later, Xi Jin's baby was finally born. It was on the very day of the Global United Memorial Day, and every city in the world was holding various activities to celebrate, including garden parties, parades with floats, and robot exhibitions. At night, the streets were filled with people setting off fireworks. The flying saucers changed colors and performed all sorts of maneuvers in formation.

United Memorial Day was held to commemorate a great individual of the last century—Max Kristen. At the time, under his leadership, a laboratory code-named Giant Star miraculously developed a mysterious element known as Nanning that was capable of neutralizing all forms of nuclear weapons. The element had unlimited power and could consume all other forms of energy. On account of this, it wasn't long before the entire world united under the name of Nanning, and Max Kristen along with a number of other national leaders organized a transnational committee. The committee was successful in channeling everything related to politics, the economy, the military, manpower, and the distribution and scientific development of resources from all parts of the world into the Nanning administrative system. Universally praised, Max Kristen was honored by being appointed the first chairman of the committee. It was said that because his ancestors were from Switzerland, peace was in his blood. Under Max Kristen's leadership and that of succeeding committee chairmen, a series of reforms were completed. Owing to the beneficent power of Nanning, traditional weapons were scrapped; oil fields were shut down (Nanning is vastly superior to oil); polluted rivers, lakes, and forests were reinvigorated; billions of inferior people from Africa, the Americas, and Asia mysteriously vanished; and the acquisition and allocation of resources was strictly controlled. Once the objectives for the material environment were achieved, the committee put its hand to an unprecedented plan, and on United Memorial Day, the second committee chairman solemnly announced via the global communications network that humanity was on the verge of a new age, an age of peace without conflicting views or disputes.

3

When the doctor entered the waiting room, it was already dark outside. Xi Jin stood at the window, staring out, lost in thought. Crowds thronged the boulevard as the rich and colorful celebrations took place.

"Xi Jin," said the doctor from behind, "congratulations."

"Huh? What?" Xi Jin turned as if on a spring.

"Congratulations. Mother and child are doing fine—and it's a boy," said the doctor. "However, some minor surgery will be required, just standard procedure. You'll have to wait till tomorrow to see him."

Shortly thereafter, Xi Jin sat down beside his wife's hospital bed and, holding her hand, gently said, "Thank you. It's a boy."

"But we can't see him till tomorrow."

"That's okay. Let's think of a name for him first."

"You decide," his wife said tenderly. "You're his father."

"Xi De, yes, let's call our son Xi De."

A week later, Xi Jin brought mother and child home from the hospital, and they resumed their ordinary and invariable farm life.

Xi Jin, like all fathers, placed all his hopes in his son, his only descendant. He hoped that Xi De might someday become an interstellar flying saucer pilot. It looked as if he wouldn't be disappointed. When the boy was six years old, he passed the Ministry of Education's Uniform Qualifications Inspection and Approval and was "qualified to receive a first-class education," meaning he would have the opportunity to become an elite administrator under the committee and work as an engineer, doctor, flying saucer pilot, electronics specialist, or department head. Therefore, little Xi De was enrolled in the Central Superior Academy by order of the Ministry of Education, where he received systematic training and education.

The Central Academy was located on the outskirts of Central City amid beautiful surroundings with a pleasant climate. From the school dormitory on the mountain slope, one could see the city buildings shining under the sun. All students, regardless of age, were required to reside on campus. Xi Jin and his wife took their son to the academy and were reluctant to part. Then they waited with great anticipation for the one day each month they could visit him.

There were 1,500 students at the academy, divided into 20 grades based on age. Those students who completed all 20 grades were guaranteed a meteoric rise in their chosen profession. All high-ranking members of the regional committee had been just such brilliant students. Every year at the time of the High-Ranking Administrators Holiday you would see the school pins flashing on the lapels of all VIPs in the waiting room at the Central Airport.

And so, in this perfect educational environment, little Xi De received the first-class education of a future outstanding administrator. With the precision provided by a computer, his knowledge and physical ability progressed at an astonishing speed.

Ten years passed in the blink of an eye. During that time, the Supreme Committee announced a number of accomplishments, including the establishment of the People's Database. A supercomputer at the Ministry of Security stored information on every citizen in every region of the new world, and information from train stations, bars, stores, and scenic vacation spots was continuously entered in regional computers. After being organized, classified, and deleted where necessary, the information was finally sent to the Central Ministry of Security. In short, with the establishment of the People's Database, the traditional census became a thing of the past.

Sixteen-year-old Xi De learned of this reform from the news. Two weeks later an "executive group" visited the academy. While there, they marked the back of his hand with the number AH5481. In a procedure much like that used by a plastic surgeon, a square silver tab was implanted flawlessly as if it were a new piece of skin on the back of the hand. Three months later, the committee announced the elimination of the currency system. When making a purchase or traveling, all one had to do was touch the ID Confirmation Scanner with the back of one's hand and it was done without the inconvenience of counting out money or making change.

Naturally, a whole series of reforms followed that abolished the limited trade system and a certain amount of licensed small private enterprise; and measures were taken to centralize the management of all service industries. All of this led to unrest in many regions, which was quickly suppressed by the security police. Around that time, a secret anti-Nanning organization started to become active.

4

Stooped over, Professor Kang Zaoshi swayed as he walked up the flight of steps to the classroom building. Behind him lay a well-manicured lawn embellished with a host of strangely shaped metal sculptures. Halfway up, he halted and heaved a sigh as he felt a stabbing pain in the joints of his feet. This was, of course, quite natural for someone of his age—he was eighty-seven and had been teaching at the academy for forty years. It was hard to imagine someone remaining in the same place for forty years. With this thought, he sighed softly, turned, and proceeded up the flight of steps.

The classroom building was a large brown structure of five stories. The walls of each classroom were covered with metal soundproofing and painted brown as well.

The door opened automatically as the professor entered the classroom. He placed the book under his arm beside the terminal at the master console, looked up, and said,

"Good morning, students."

"Good morning, Professor," the five students replied in unison.

Then the professor took his seat and hit a key on the keyboard in front of him. Immediately, a colorful image appeared on the screen behind him.

"Professor!" shouted one of the students. "That is the homework from two days ago."

"What's the date today?" asked the professor.

"The eighteenth."

"Ah!" The professor hit the key again, changing the image on the screen. "It's age. My memory isn't what it used to be."

"In our last class, we discussed the social structure of the late twentieth century," he began. "In those days you could say it was a time of chaos, great and utter chaos."

Xi De sat in the second row, his chin in his hand, listening intently. For some reason he was fascinated by his class on the modern history of the world. He had never missed a class and on a number of occasions he had returned to the classroom alone to review and enjoy the day's videotaped lesson.

"During the great chaos, there were thirty-four individual schools of philosophy, including pragmatism, analytical philosophy, existentialism, socialism, and communism; there were sixty-four large international organizations, including the United Nations, the Warsaw Pact, NATO, OPEC, and ASEAN, among others; there were also various forms of government—around fifty in all—including democracy, partial democracy, constitutional monarchy, totalitarianism, communism, and mixed communism and capitalism."

Xi De listened quietly as a series of disturbing images appeared one after another on the screen: cheering crowds, military parades, war, famine, hospitals, the megalomania on the faces of politicians, impassioned speeches, piles of corpses, atomic bomb blasts, and other frightening, cruel, and absurd scenes. What kind of a world was it? He wondered how it compared with the world today. Without a doubt it was a barbaric and dark age.

"The world in those days had a population of four billion people living under a cloud of destruction, living under a terrible threat. . . ."

The film continued to roll—one dismembered body followed by many.

"Various forms of drugs provided brief escape from the world. They included opium, morphine, marijuana, and LSD. In addition, there were hundreds of religious organizations that served as an opiate. Let us pause here. This is Guyana, where a nuclear reaction test lab was located. At the time, there was a religious organization called the People's Church. One night, the five hundred fanatical members of the group committed suicide because they actually thought they would go to Heaven."

That was history; the tragic and insane history of humanity. Xi De replayed the earlier visual feed. He couldn't bear to keep watching. He discovered that everyone else was the same.

The professor remained silent for a while, then shook his head and turned off the screen.

"But that wasn't the problem," said the professor, his low voice calling everyone's attention back to him.

"The problem was that there was no power, system, or theory that could solve the predicament. At the time, a famous sociologist provided a clear description of the situation in these terms: 'what we see before us is a comprehensive industrial crisis that transcends the conflict between capitalism and Soviet Communism. It is a crisis that has undermined the foundation of our resources, system of values, perception of time and space, and identity, as well as the economy.' What you see before you is the complete collapse of industrial civilization."

As he listened to the professor's voice, an ever clearer picture took shape in Xi De's mind. He realized to his astonishment that it was the very image of Max Kristen. Right! It was him, Max Kristen. Huge photos of him were hung in the most conspicuous locations in all public places, offices, and factories. His shining eyes shone with the light of profound wisdom; his face, with its sharp features, conveyed confidence, firmness, and moral courage. Right! There was no doubt about it. It was Max Kristen, the great Max Kristen, a beacon of light in a dark age of fear and hopelessness, as the textbooks described him. He was the one who led all of mankind out of that insane and suffocating nightmare.

The class finally ended on an unbearably uncomfortable note.

"Professor," asked Xi De, running up to the professor as he was about to leave the classroom, "why were the people of the twentieth century so stupid?"

"Stupid? Oh, they weren't stupid at all."

"Then why would anyone take themselves to the brink of extinction?"

"That's the inevitable result."

"But Nanning, but if Nanning had not appeared . . ."

"Perhaps extinction, perhaps not . . ."

"But you just said that humanity was on the brink of extinction. It was certainly Max Kristen who rescued the world."

"'Brink' does not imply the end. Perhaps the great chaos was the prerequisite for great stability. Max Kristen changed the world."

"Professor, why do you say 'changed' and not 'rescued'?"

The professor made no reply. Xi De watched as he departed, silently shrugging his shoulders. Perhaps, due to his age, his thoughts were not that clear. Xi De could not imagine what sort of a world it would be if not for Max Kristen and Nanning. Perhaps humanity would still be killing, until the last person was dead.

He was seventeen, on the verge of becoming a young man. But his education had made him superior to most people. Graduates of the Central Superior Academy were the cream of the new world. His parents often bragged about him to the neighbors. Wrapped in thought, Xi De walked back to the dorm. It would soon be lunchtime. He scrutinized the number AH5481 on the back of his hand. AH was the prefix of the high-ranking administrators of the district and was highly respected throughout society. All he had to do was stay focused on his studies and he could guarantee that one day he would enter the Administrative Department of Central City. If he performed well, he could enjoy vacation time, savoring the pleasures of traveling the firmament. That was the most cherished desire of his father, who was a farmer, and one Xi De would gladly accomplish for him.

5

Since questioning his professor, Xi De had taken a strong interest in that white-haired old man. So he began paying frequent visits to the professor at his residence in the faculty and staff dorm at dusk.

The dorms consisted of rows of exquisite two-story buildings facing a clear man-made river and the distant view of the peaceful green mountains.

In the book-filled rooms where the old man lived (strangely, he didn't own a television), the two of them developed a father-and-son relationship. While his classmates were tirelessly studying, applying themselves in preparation for making a contribution to the new world, Xi De acquired the habit of whiling away an entire evening in the old professor's house. Xi De always helped the old man make tea; then they would play various interesting forms of ancient chess. Beneath an antique clock, time seemed to go back several decades. Sometimes they would go to the storeroom and the professor would remove from a box several wooden sculptures or various metal ornaments ravaged by time. One statue of the Mile Buddha in particular seemed to hold an interesting religious tale. Sometimes the professor would offer some historical artifacts omitted from the textbooks. But each time Xi De wanted to delve more deeply into an issue, the professor would change the subject, as if discussing such things was forbidden.

"Professor," said Xi De, unable to restrain himself from asking, "have you always been alone?"

The setting sun shone through the window onto the professor's wrinkled brow.

"Ha, Xi De," the professor replied, laughing softly. "I'm accustomed to being alone, and now there's you."

"But Professor, how can one get by, cut off from the rest of the world?"

"First, he must be at the end of his life," said the professor, his eyes narrowing to slits. "Second, he must teach the dying subject of history in this damnable place."

"How can it be dying?"

"In the new world, no one is interested in the past, because there is no time to look back. Xi De, history is becoming an archive to be consulted only when there is a need. If something has no practical value, it has no reason to exist."

"But—"

"Let's not talk about it," said the professor, cutting Xi De short. "How is your class work these days?"

"The school wants me to specialize in resource analysis."

"Resource analysis is a course that requires that you only complete the sixteenth level of study."

"My grades haven't been very good. I can't study any course to the twentieth level or beyond."

"What level are you at now?"

"The thirteenth," replied Xi De. "I can graduate in another three years."

"That's too bad," said the professor as he picked up his teacup and took a sip. "Just keep at it; being a resource analyst isn't bad."

"I don't understand it— since last year, I haven't been able to focus."

"You're different from the other young people." He paused for several seconds, his burning eyes resting on Xi De. "You have intelligence."

"Intelligence, what's that?"

"It's something natural that humanity is on the verge of losing, and it would take too long to explain."

Confused, Xi De stared at the professor. Xi De felt he was in the presence of an enigmatic abyss, difficult to comprehend. In the classroom, all questions were answered with reasonable explanations. Higher education did not allow the students to go to bed with any doubts. The instructors wanted you to use a computer in your deliberations, because it could provide answers to all questions as well as assist you in selecting the most accurate answer. Intuition, premonitions, and impulse were proven in the tenth level of education to be a waste of time, irrational, and unscientific. In a highly advanced organization, a mistake in judgment was the most unforgivable of crimes.

In one simple but effective experiment, they had Xi De swallow a pill in a small room. The pill, it was said, could stimulate a certain part of the brain and, after a brief moment, allow him to experience the illusion of floating. No, it was not an illusion! He really saw himself flying in the sky, the blue sea beneath his feet. Flying into a gust of wind, his cheeks smarted, struck by the high-speed atoms of air. Afterward, when he came to his senses, they let him watch the video made while he was hallucinating. He saw with his own eyes that from start to finish, he'd been in that small room, his arms spread, flapping them the way a bird flaps its wings and making all kinds of comical movements.

"We'd rather trust our instruments," concluded the lab instructor.

6

With the strict, precise, and intellectual education that he had received, young Xi De possessed the necessary technical and specialized knowledge to become a resource analyst. In other words, he finally became an envied administrator. In June, he passed his exams for graduation while the classmates with whom he had entered the academy continued on to the seventeenth level. They shook hands with him, their voices totally devoid of any feeling.

Jin Yisheng, the dean, summoned Xi De to his office.

"Don't be too discouraged because you cannot pursue advanced studies," said the dean, trying to comfort him. "Max Kristen said that the society of the future needs all sorts of talented people. As with a construction crane, every part, every screw must be intact—it's not just the joystick that is important."

After saying good-bye to the dean, Xi De proceeded to Professor Kang's room and knocked on his door.

The sound of coughing came from behind the door.

"Professor, are you all right?"

"I've got a bit of a cold. It doesn't matter. Come in."

"I came to say good-bye," said Xi De. "I graduated."

They sat down in the living room. Professor Kang, who was dressed in pajamas, poured tea for him as usual.

"Time flies. I remember when you were this small," said the old man, gesturing with his hand. "It's strange. I've taught so many students, but so few ever come to say good-bye to me."

Tears welled up in the professor's eyes as Xi De watched, astonished.

"What's the matter, Professor?"

"I'm so touched." He raised his hand to dry his eyes. "Xi De, I think you will encounter all sorts of unexpected troubles in the future. I shouldn't have told you so many things about the 'past.'"

"Nonsense, Professor," said Xi De, "you have made me more 'intelligent.'"

The word made them laugh.

"Well," said the old man, "I have nothing to give you. These antiques of mine are of no use to you. But I have some things to say that I hope you will remember after you leave school. Don't tell anyone about the two of us. You must also be observant, but don't ask questions, and keep a distance from others. If you have the opportunity, you can come and visit me. That's enough, Xi De, you'd better get going and pack your things."

7

The Bureau of Resource Analysis was a level-two unit attached to the Ministry of Resources.

Xi De's office faced the towering government administrative building. Whether for its imposing nature or its gorgeous exterior, the building had undoubtedly become the symbol of Central City. Xi De often stepped to the window and gazed at the enormous silver structure. On clear days, rays of sunlight would shimmer within his four walls, exuding a charismatic power. He could see nothing else from his window but the government administrative building. His was a small but fully appointed office. He also had two female office assistants. In addition, there was a neat row of stern-looking and forbidding machines, including computers for receiving, dispatching, and analysis. It was Xi De's job to collect production figures from a given region and, after compiling and organizing them, to produce analytical charts and graphs. The work required utilizing a number of different machines, which occupied most of his time. The moment he felt he could relax a little, he'd step over to the beverage machine, where he'd pour himself a cup of tea or coffee, and then step back over to the window and gaze out at the apparently unchanging scene until he experienced a slight feeling of disgust, after which he would walk over to the desks of the two female assistants and chat with them about anything and everything.

Aqing and Senni were both outstanding students from the Intermediate Academy. Both were petite and quite attractive. They loved to talk about school life as if it were the only topic worth discussing. The academy specialized in training office staff such as assistants and secretaries. Their special skills included speed reading, typing, counting, and following orders. The curriculum at the Intermediate Academy was superficial compared to that of the Superior Academy, while the discipline was much stricter (the Superior Academy took a much more relaxed attitude when it came to extracurricular activities). On this particular day, they proudly told Xi De about how the braver girls hopped the wall and left the school at night. But judging from the clever gleam in their eyes, it was apparent that they were, in fact, bragging.

"What did you do when you went out so late?" Xi De couldn't help asking. The streets were empty at night save for in the amusement districts, and students going out for a stroll on the streets was just inconceivable.

"We didn't do anything; we just wanted to get out."

Xi De grunted, ending the conversation, and returned to his desk. He lowered his head and focused on his forms for reporting statistics. He didn't look up again until the music indicating the end of the workday sounded. He put the charts and graphs on his desk in the drawer, walked over to the receiver and switched it to automatic, turned off the data-processing computer, said good-bye to the two young ladies, and left.

In the elevator, he was accosted by another resource analyst by the name of Lin Xing.

"Hey, let's go have a drink." Lin was tall and thin and had been at the bureau for five years.

They entered the bar on the ground floor of the building together. At that time, the bar was crowded with employees wearing Ministry of Resources insignias on their lapels. Xi De made his way through the crowd to the bar, where he ordered two glasses of green wine, a pungent, fiery liquor. As the bartender handed him the glasses, he also pushed a small metal box toward him. Xi De touched it with the back of his hand, paying for the drinks.

"I prefer money, especially those old copper coins," said Lin Xing. "When you drop a handful of coppers on the bar and hear them ring, now that's music to the ears."

"Abolishing the currency system was progress," replied Xi De casually. "The age of opinion is a thing of the past; talking about such things is a waste of time."

They fell silent. Xi De looked around at the noisy crowd. There were several tables of men and women that seemed to form a loud group. A fat guy with a red face was mouthing a popular song.

There is no past, there is no future,
There is nothing but the present for us.
There is no sadness, there is no happiness,
There is nothing but indifference for us.
There is no argument, there is no splitting,
There is nothing but work for us.

The song faded amid a burst of raucous laughter. Xi De looked away and clinked glasses with Lin Xing.

"What do you think?" asked Lin. "You've been here almost six months. What do you think?"

"It's all right. I don't have anything to worry about."

"Of course you don't have anything to worry about." Lin laughed grimly. "There'll come a day when they'll replace you with a machine."

"Lin, you're drunk."

"I'm not drunk, but I can't go to bed," he said draining his glass. "See that guy over there? He's drinking because he is unhappy."

"That's not good," said Xi De, shaking his head. "It'll have an impact on his efficiency."

"Old chap," said Lin, pressing closer, "efficiency exists only in the high-level departments. You must know that."

It's classic job fatigue, thought Xi De. Perhaps Lin Xing needed a vacation. Of course, as the books said, in a highly specialized society, people must have the appropriate occupation or the slightest change would create waste. Fatigue and exhaustion are normal physiological phenomena, but how to solve the resultant loss of efficiency and how to restore one's original work ethic had become the focus of the Bureau of Character Readjustment within the Ministry of Education.

"How long has it been since your last vacation?"

"Old chap," said Lin Xing, looking at him strangely, "I know what you are thinking, so I won't talk about it anymore with you."

8

Xi De returned to the singles dorm of the Resource Analysis Bureau, which consisted of perfect apartments like a honeycomb occupying the top floors of the building. They contained all sorts of automatic conveniences to the extent that if you needed some article of daily use, all you had to do was touch the computer keyboard. In a matter of minutes the article would be delivered directly to you via a conduit door in the wall. This way of life was superior to the farm life of Xi De's parents. He once brought his parents to the dormitory and was deeply moved by the expressions of pride they felt for their son. Such affection was rarely encountered. In a fixed job, people moved at a fixed pace and rarely had time for others.

Still dressed, Xi De fell on his bed. The effect of the wine seemed to have increased. With his hands clasped behind his head, he began to give free rein to his thoughts. Lin Xing's words made him a little uncomfortable. Over the last few months, he had grown accustomed to the regular order of everything. When something out of the ordinary occurred, it left him feeling alarmed. He would recall the elderly professor at school and how he could actually conjure up the past. But of what use was it? According to the laws of nature, it served only to obstruct the flow of progress. The entire new society was in the process of moving forward, just as Max Kristen said: "Rapid progress will soon leave all problems behind. To pause is to perish."

According to the standard education he had received, less the influence of the old professor, he was but one force in the forward progress of society as a whole. Therefore, the individual will could not be suffered to exist; one had to sacrifice oneself for the greater good. Only if every element advanced uniformly in the same direction would it do any good. If one element deviated, the damage caused . . .

I can't think this way again, thought Xi De vaguely.

Then he fell asleep. A peculiar picture, gray and static, appeared out of the haze before his eyes. It looked coldly at Xi De as he dreamed. The picture was of an abandoned field (owing to superfluous production one year), stripped tree trunks, cracked mud, and a dry well.

The picture accompanied him throughout the long night. The next morning, Xi De blinked forcefully, dispelling the illusion and, without giving it much thought beyond feeling a little strange, resumed his tranquil, unvarying daily life.

There were no changes worth mentioning in his office; order was strictly controlled, which is to say there had been no technical problems. Analysis of the output of Number Three Industrial City: Normal. Number Four Industrial City: Normal. Number Five. . . . The two female assistants were discussing the big story in the morning's news. The Supreme Committee had announced an accomplishment worth celebrating: a bio lab had managed to successfully develop a means of reproducing life from a human cell without the need for sexual reproduction. It was predicted that this experiment would ultimately lead to the elimination of the old-style and moribund family system. In the foreseeable future, the father and mother of humanity would be the new society, and each person would no longer be anyone's emotional burden. He could loudly proclaim without any emotional conflict: "I love my organization; I love my society."

Thus these assistants, this generation of young people would never be troubled by the moral difficulties of marriage. Xi De himself was no exception. Although he understood the lifestyle of the previous generation better than most, still, he basically believed that a perfect society was an absolutely rational society and that love and marriage were replete with irrationality. (His sixteen years of intellectual training had not been a waste.) Passionate and childish relations between the sexes and emotional imbalance would be excised forever from the human character in the new society.

After a day in the office, Xi De returned directly to the dorm, turned on the television, and watched an entertainment show. It had been two weeks since he had gone out. Anyway, there wasn't anything to do except go someplace for entertainment—a bar, theater, or pool hall. Therefore you never saw anyone out for a spin. In fact, when it came to all the former establishments for life's needs—small, privately run shops and restaurants and simple services—if they hadn't died out, they had merged into huge and uniform centers. Your office was in the floor above or below you; likewise, the amusement parlors, bars, and restaurants were all in the same building. In some places, the Resource Building for example, you never had to set foot outside the door your entire life if you didn't want to. Naturally, if you wanted to smooth out the emotional imbalance created by a boring, monotonous life (and this had already been thoroughly considered), the new society allowed you to take a vacation or travel for a while. A proper itinerary would be arranged for you and there would be no unnecessary waste—getting lost, delays in obtaining accommodations, lost time, and other evils.

At nine o'clock, Xi De received a phone call from his father to say that his mother had been ill but had already seen a doctor and was taking medication. Xi De told his father that he would be home on Sunday, then hung up and continued watching television.

There was a historical drama on. The characters consisted of a group of people from the old world who were scrambling for wealth and power. Bloody coups, bloodless coups, revolutions, protests, rebellion, elections through bribery, corruption, think tanks run by business, mass media at the service of tyrants working to oppress the masses. So-called democracies were nothing but a bunch of political schemers; communist countries did nothing but play with complicated class conflicts. The result would clearly be a pestilent war. The drama was a farce from start to finish, including its hackneyed and solemn theme. Fortunately, at the last minute a great epoch-making individual appeared (of course, the viewers all knew who this great individual was) to put an end to the chaos. As the sound of laughter rose from the screen, Xi De switched off the television. He sat comfortably on the sofa and poured himself a cup of tea. He took an old copy of *Resource Newsletter* out of a drawer and flipped through it absentmindedly. When he turned to the last page, where outstanding workers were introduced, he was surprised to find Lin Xing listed there. The article cited Lin's efficient performance over the years and with some humor announced his year-end efficiency award. In addition to a trip to the North Pole, he also received a special prize—an android beauty. Reading this, Xi De couldn't help but laugh—this sort of man-made sexual companion was extremely expensive, not something everyone could afford. But many people would rather have one of them than get married. It appeared Lin Xing had everything, but then why was he so unhappy?

Closing the newsletter, Xi De sighed. The questions school had been unable to answer slowly arose in his mind, followed by images of his worry-free days at the Central Academy. A short time later, he went to bed.

Like the night before, that strange face, gray and static, appeared in his dream, the only difference this time being that it was accompanied by an oppressive metallic voice that seemed to repeat the same thing: "Come here, come here, something awaits you."

The following morning, Xi De sat in bed mulling over the dream of the night before. He knew the psychological explanation of a dream, but this one was very peculiar and real, and he'd dreamed the same thing two times. Today's parapsychology had a relatively comprehensive theory holding that the power of the human mind is a form of energy. Twenty years earlier, the great psychologist Fan Keqiang had performed a famous experiment. Electric shocks of ten thousand volts were repeatedly applied to the brain of a volunteer. As the electricity flowed, the vision of the test subject could actually penetrate walls and see what was on the other side.

Well, how was he to explain his dream? Xi De sat in bed thinking for a while, but came up with no ideas.

The next night, the strange dream and the metallic sound appeared a third time. Xi De woke with a start around midnight. He threw on his clothes, sat down on the sofa, and struggled to recall the dream. Finally, he picked up a pencil and drew what he had seen in his dream on a piece of paper. The moment he laid aside his pencil, he realized that there was something very familiar about the drawing. Then he began to search his memory and did so until daybreak.

9

On Sunday morning, Xi De caught the electric bus to the Number Two Agricultural City. He carried gifts for his family that he had purchased at the Daily Goods Center, including a nice razor, a high-frequency massager, and box of powdered wine. There were several times more cars on the road than usual; the many-colored buildings shone brightly under the sun. As the bus entered a blue highway overpass, the scenery changed—forests gave way to hills, which gave way to barren, open countryside, but there was not a building in sight. Occasionally several wild animals would appear on the barren wastes and two children on the bus would shout with excitement. Xi De closed his eyes to sleep, but that dream that had been haunting him for three days reappeared in his mind's eye.

I've got it! Xi De almost shouted aloud. That place, that place in the dream, he remembered now. That mysterious place was near the family farm, just on the other side of a hill. It was abandoned farmland, a remnant of land reform and a redrawing of boundaries that was carried out after crop overproduction. The overproduction had resulted in a vicious cycle of wasted resources. As a result of redrawing the boundaries, a certain percentage of farmers changed occupations and became road workers, which it was said led to a small workers' demonstration.

After lunch, Xi De told his parents he wanted to go for a walk in the fields. Out under the warm noon sun, he headed toward that mysterious place that had been beckoning him.

The green fields were covered with square fiberglass structures; the field rows were clear of weeds. A small mechanical harvester rested in a shed. Xi De climbed the hill and passed through a forest, and then the abandoned fields suddenly appeared before his eyes.

He couldn't help slowing his pace, advancing nervously. He felt strange crossing the dry soil crisscrossed with a spiderweb of cracks. That metallic voice seemed to call to him: "Come here, come here. Something awaits you."

Xi De scanned all around, but aside from the cracked rice fields and withered trees, there wasn't anything to offend the eye. But as he scanned the area again, a round object caught his attention. That's it! It was the ancient well of the abandoned field, covered with an overgrowth of weeds. Xi De peered in and saw that there was something among the weeds at the bottom of the well. After hesitating for a moment, he climbed down into the well. When he climbed out, he was carrying a metal box.

Several terrifying scenes from sci-fi movies flashed through his mind. His shock and curiosity reached a peak simultaneously. So he opened the box.

It was a book, a strange book. Xi De let out a cry.

The cover of the book had yellowed; it looked as if it were made of animal skin. The binding was of an inferior quality, certainly not made in the present century.

Xi De sat by the mouth of the well, flabbergasted. Nothing was stirring and not a cloud was seen in the sky. The open space seemed to conceal a mysterious but palpable force.

He opened the book.

THE TRUE FACE OF THE SUPREME COMMITTEE
By Winston

I am sixty-eight this year. Given the medical advances of today, that is an insignificant age. But I suffer from an illness and know that my time among the living is limited, perhaps another three months. It is a disease for which the medical community as yet has no name. After they announced a cure for cancer, the last enemy of humankind, this illness became a joke of sorts. Three months. What should a man who has only three months left to live do?

Perhaps everyone would give a different answer. But as for me, I rejoice at finally coming to a point in time when I must face myself. I believe I have a responsibility to evaluate my life in the most objective and impartial fashion. And more importantly: I must tell myself the truth.

I served as secretary of the Supreme Committee for thirty years. In those thirty years, I participated in humanity's final, earth-shaking, and violent changes. Not only that, but I was privileged to share in a secret the public will never know about. If I hadn't been afflicted with this mortal illness, perhaps this secret would have been swallowed by the torrent of time. Of all the people who participated in these events, including Max Kristen, no one but me has experienced this, called "one of the activities of the degenerated human intelligence—the process of the struggle of conscience." I lost my family during the violent changes. Originally, this suffering was compensated for by a sublime ideal, meaning that in those days I transferred my cherished feelings to the great mission of "leading humanity into the new age." But in these last three months, the final days of my life, I feel I have lost the ability to cheat myself and others any longer. I must speak, I must speak....

The great Max Kristen, who will be treated as a divinity by generations to come, was, in fact, a villain, a swindler. He was an insane idealist. And the Supreme Committee was a violent, cruel, and bloody organization.

Reading to this point, Xi De had to close the book. He heaved a great sigh, as if the violent shock were too much for him. After a while, he continued reading.

I daresay that anyone who has read to this point will have to look away or experience a subconscious conflict. In any case, please be patient and continue to read. Unmasking a universally accepted lie or overturning an irreplaceable idol will produce something akin to a mental collapse. And as for myself? Well, when I say these things, I experience an almost laughable sense of committing a crime. After all, the Supreme Committee and Max Kristen occupied an important place in my life, and suddenly to deny them is not only tantamount to a crime but also disillusionment with life.

The first time I met Max Kristen was one week after I had joined the secretariat. That was in 1997. The secretariat was located in New York and subordinate to the Nanning Committee. At the time, no one had a clear understanding of the committee. Even Congress knew only that the secretariat was directly responsible to the President of the United States in an official and unofficial capacity. Prior to this I was the South African representative to the United Nations Committee on Racial Discrimination. South Africa was a rich and beautiful country, but also a place that was criticized by the rest of the world. Outsiders, however, didn't necessarily understand its true internal situation. Many large nations that had achieved "racial equality" actually suffered from the worst racial discrimination. After an especially heated debate, I lost all confidence in the UN Committee on Racial Discrimination. You could say that I was totally disheartened. So I packed my bags and was ready to go home to my family and country. It was at this time that a member of Nanning approached me and asked if I would be interested in working for them. It was the first time I had ever heard of an organization called the Nanning Committee.

I don't know why, but I was persuaded to work first and decide later, so I stayed in New York and within a week met Max Kristen.

I can still clearly remember Max Kristen's appearance, because in thirty years he never changed.

"I understand the difficulties you have encountered," he said, looking at me with kind, paternal eyes. He was forty or fifty at the time, ruddy complexioned, and with facial features that left a deep impression on everyone. "But this problem was solved by Darwin ages ago."

As he spoke, his eyes were fixed on mine, carefully examining my facial expressions.

Following which, he began to redefine the word "human being." Today, thirty years later, when I recall his words, my hair stands on end. History has no shortage of such precedents in which the words of one giant at a certain time have a frightening influence on society, so much so that a single word can result in a river of blood.

The ultimate aim of the human species, according to Max Kristen, setting aside its origins, was to become the highest organism. Accordingly, the significance of its existence was to continuously eliminate any and all obstacles to its progress, such as physiological decline, mental degeneration, and all inherited defects. No price was too great to pay for achieving the goal of human perfection. There was absolutely nothing new to this argument. Many people had advocated the same thing, but all they had done was talk. At the time, I naturally agreed with him; the population pressures on the world were becoming greater and resources were becoming scarcer. The populations in highly developed countries were controlled, while those in less developed countries were out of control. This led to what is termed the issue of "less desirable populations." The slightest accomplishments of civilization were unable to bear the pressures of overpopulation. Our ancestors solved this problem through war. It was a simple solution: all that had to be done was select the preferred place for the battlefield. But once modern atomic warfare exploded on the scene, battlefield factors meant little or nothing—the first to be affected were the scientifically advanced nations. After one such war, the only survivors would possibly be the primitive peoples of the Amazonian rain forests. These half-wit savages were a joke compared to a highly intelligent organism capable of space travel.

Max Kristen, however, wasn't so explicit. In the beginning he merely hinted. The situation at the time had reached an imminent crisis. Many small nations possessed nuclear arms but maintained a cavalier attitude, as if not fully realizing that such weapons could blow the earth to smithereens. For this reason, the superpowers grew concerned that recklessness on the part of one small country could result in a global nuclear holocaust. The United States had been cognizant of this problem ten years earlier. A lab code-named Giant Star was born. After ten years of concerted effort, they developed a new weapon called Nanning. It was a mysterious and terrifying device. Deployed in space, it was capable of destroying any nuclear weapon on the face of the earth.

At this point, Xi De paused for a moment to think. The mysterious constructive element mentioned in the textbooks was then, in fact, nothing more than a detonation device.

It was only six months after I joined the secretariat that I learned the secret of Nanning. At the time, more than two hundred people were employed there, one third Germans, a small number of Asians, and the rest Americans. Max Kristen was Swiss, though this was doubtful. Strangely, there were no Jews or blacks. Owing to intelligence considerations, I have no way of ascertaining the composition of the Supreme Committee or executive organizations. The duties of my job—global racial analysis—were very complicated. I had to assemble materials on the bloodlines and cultures of more than one thousand races and then organize, arrange, analyze, evaluate, and submit the results to the committee.

Three years after I joined the secretariat, Pakistan detonated its first atomic bomb. The UN immediately announced sanctions. Rumors emanated from all parts of the globe, but none implicating Nanning. Afterward a series of mysterious nuclear detonations occurred periodically. The world succumbed to extreme hysteria and all countries grew suspicious of one another. The UN, for its part, seemed to be half in a stupor, and all international activities ground to a halt. In addition, natural disasters, earthquakes, tsunamis, droughts, and plagues came in quick succession, due to environmental degradation. The Soviet Union was on the point of collapse. The United States was accused of being responsible, but there was no sufficient proof, so it flatly denied any responsibility. But what was its response to the unending series of human catastrophes? According to *The New York Times*, the leading newspaper of the day, "The White House called for all Americans to remain calm in the midst of the chaos." The American president appeared frequently on television, accompanied by a number of high-level technical consultants, who criticized the disasters caused by the "small nuclear states" as "serious technological errors." They believed that the manufacture of nuclear weapons was not difficult, but there was much to learn in the management of them. Then Max Kristen appeared at the president's side. I recall it was the first time he spoke publicly. His speech was moving and rousing. The following day, all newspapers without exception carried his speech and heaped praise on him. In those days, Max Kristen was Chairman of the White House Committee on Science and Technology. However, rumor in the secretariat had it that the president was already under his control. Max Kristen declared that the series of disasters represented a turning point in the history of human civilization. A ray, emanating from somewhere deep in the universe, had detonated the stockpiled nuclear weapons. It was a warning to humanity about the careless use of these ultimate weapons. "We sorrow for and are deeply grieved by the plight of the people in the disaster areas. Each and every one of us has a responsibility to look ahead to the future and to continue the as yet uncompleted mission of humanity." It was precisely at that time that Max Kristen issued his "View of Human History," after which he described the beautiful prospects in a disaster area after rebuilding. The explosion had overturned everything, which bestowed on us a *tabula rasa*, a new land filled with hope. What remained for us to do was to get rid of the remaining atomic dust and initiate a new beginning for humanity. Following this, he announced in all seriousness the Nanning Committee, proclaiming it the "fountainhead of the future happiness of mankind." Afterward the committee gradually expanded and eventually came to replace the UN. Max Kristen's power also increased. He made the contaminated land productive again as well as gathering together the refugees who had fled elsewhere (these included the cream of the place—the government officials, teachers, doctors, engineers, and the rich and powerful), and then, as he saw fit, reestablished the homeland.

10

It gradually grew dark. The overwhelming scene began to reveal a gentle, yielding, and calm side as the veil of night descended all around. Sitting beside the well, Xi De gently clasped the book, immersing himself in the magical moment as day gave way to night.

The vacuum left in his soul after such a great shock slowly receded, but fear, confusion, and uneasiness swept in to replace it. His first thought was that if the book wasn't a plot of some sort, it must have been scribbled by a madman. There was just no way that the new world, perfect and filled with hope as it was, could be the result of a mad and bloody plot as described by Winston. Winston had to be a lunatic, bored or delusional.

Xi De stood up, exhaled, and set off toward home.

"Xi De," said his father at the dinner table with a note of concern, "aren't you feeling well?"

"I'm fine," he replied.

Unable to sleep, Xi De got out of bed around midnight. His mind was running wild like a three-ring circus—a form of amusement from the old society that no longer existed. You learned of these things by finding them mentioned in books or seeing them in old movies. Of course other things had disappeared too, such as the nonsense about which Winston had written. Why? Because the new society was filled with so many rational, wise, and useful things. And people? What had happened to 90 percent of the population? Those billions of people just like you with a brain, two eyes, and a pair of ears—what happened to them? Winston offered an explanation; the textbooks offered a different explanation. Winston offered a nonsensical explanation, while the textbooks offered a rational explanation with proof. No! Not an explanation, but rather the truth. *But there has to be a reason for someone to go to so much trouble to write this book and then come to tell me about it a half century later in a dream.*

Xi De sat at his desk facing the book, mulling over this mysterious and incomprehensible matter. After fifteen minutes, he just had to open the book.

Winston followed with an extremely detailed description of his major works on the committee. At the same time, he provided numbers that only reinforced the veracity of the book. Winston mentioned a small island called Light of the Pacific, which was the previous name of the tenth regional committee under which Xi De served. Sixty or seventy years earlier, after Nanning had obliterated everything on the island, a reconstruction project was drafted. The plan proposed the establishment of five industrial cities and three agricultural cities (in this he was correct). But then it was possible to forge things simply by altering the dates. This was an important point of doubt. As Xi De read, he noted the dubious points on a piece of paper. He simply noted them without knowing how he was going to handle them. There were several other points of doubt: Was the unusual dream that summoned him a plot on someone's part? If that was indeed the case, then why seek out someone as insignificant as himself? And what was the point of it all? How could a denouncement transcend time and space and occur in his head?

Following this, Winston mentioned how Max Kristen became a global superstar by handling most of Russia and part of the United States. The destructive character of Nanning began to undergo a change as well— another of its functions was its ability to quickly eliminate atomic fallout and provide once again a piece of virgin land unsullied by human hands. And so Max Kristen and his working group would appear at the "land of miracles" like Moses in Exodus. Finally, one day, a transnational committee was born, either because it was needed to help the work group accomplish its goals or because those who had survived the catastrophe needed a model spiritual symbol. Max Kristen, of course, was honored with appointment as first chairman.

The last few sections of the book described Winston's family and his road to enlightenment. On the last page of the book, Winston penned one line: "In my soul, I humbly pray for the forgiveness of humankind."

Soft music floated from the home computer. Xi De knew that a new day had dawned. He left his desk and pulled open the curtains. The gentle light of the sun pierced his tired eyes. He hadn't slept all night.

11

As always, the machines in the Bureau of Resource Analysis were functioning smoothly. But Xi De's heart had undergone a change of sorts. He had departed from the perfect work life that had been arranged for him. He had begun to make contact with the outside world in a spirit of curiosity, uncertainty, and alertness.

One Sunday afternoon, Xi De set off for the Central Academy he had long since left. The chaste and elegant dorms, the refreshing gardens, and the students who held themselves aloof from the world all stirred warm memories.

Professor Kang Zaoshi opened the door and, startled, looked upon this student who had long since grown up.

"Professor," said Xi De in that old-style living room, "I've missed you."

The old man nodded and poured him a cup of tea. Xi De noticed his trembling, age-spotted hands.

"You have grown up. How are you doing?"

"That's hard to say—there are still many things I have not experienced."

"Don't be in any hurry," said the professor, sitting opposite him, looking him over with his kind eyes. "How's your job?"

Xi De then began to tell him about his work at the Bureau of Resource Analysis. The old man nodded from time to time.

After Xi De finished speaking, the old man smiled by way of conclusion. Then he stood up and invited Xi De to accompany him to the garden to look at his flowers.

"One day, these beautiful plants will disappear without a trace," said the old man as he walked.

"Why is that?"

"The concept of beauty is in the process of changing. In the future, people will only have eyes for space or the products of science and technology."

"Oh."

They paused before a rose in full bloom.

"Look at how touching these flowers are," said the old man. "I've devoted so much time and energy to growing them."

"Professor, why not just use a growth formula? In a matter of weeks you'd have a garden filled with roses."

"That's not the same. These flowers, like people, have lives. Do you understand, Xi De? You can't rush a living organism to make it grow faster."

"Why not? There are limits to a person's life. Why waste so much time on education?"

"When you reach my age, you'll understand. Sometimes I regret missing many things because I was in such a hurry."

Xi De grunted noncommittally. They resumed walking. The professor paused beneath an oddly shaped pine tree.

"Xi De, you didn't come here to chat, did you?"

Xi De shook his head. Then he began to relate the recent series of events, beginning with the dream he'd had three days in a row and leading to his uncertainties. He poured out his heart to the professor without leaving out a detail, great or small.

The minutes passed as Xi De told his story. The professor listened intently and when the story ended, he whispered to Xi De, "Let's go inside."

The slanting rays of the setting sun poured through the living room window. In all seriousness, the old professor fixed his eyes on the pure and puzzled face of the young man and said, "It's hard to believe that you actually ran into this sort of thing in this age, this century. If there were such a thing as fate, then you'd have been duped by it. There is no reason that the violent changes of the last century should have anything to do with you. Your class origin, your own background, in fact nothing about you should obviate Winston from choosing you. That is, if Winston really existed. He's a complete bungler if he throws everything into crossing space and time looking for someone to redeem him and then manages to find a big child like you, so pure and innocent. It's a bad joke.

"I have not heard about most of the things Winston describes. However, the truthfulness of some of what he says I can confirm, based on my own experience. This ought to be of use to you, but how much I can't say. Perhaps the whole thing is nothing but a harmless prank or nothing more than a history lesson. People these days are not interested in history mainly because it has already taken shape. In a civilization that has taken shape and is heading for its zenith, history has nothing of interest to offer, and no one has time to look at the past, especially in today's age of superscience and technology. The issues faced by 99 percent of people these days will not be resolved by looking at the past. The challenges of the future transcend the sum total of a few thousand years of human history. At the beginning of the twentieth century, when Henry Ford produced his first Model T, the cave paintings of primitive man were nothing more than a topic for an interesting chat. Likewise, Marx's political theories, when run through our computers today, will be seen as no more than childish scrawl. The study of history has evolved into what it is not because of the shortcomings of certain individuals but because it has become a kind of mechanically applied specialized jargon, a 'historical necessity.' After teaching history for forty years in the academy, I have come to one conclusion: it has less practical value than literature. And what is the fate of literature these days? But this has nothing to do with what we are talking about. I want to tell you my personal experience. It might help to explain some of what has happened to you.

"Sixty years ago—a long, long time ago—when I was only twenty-seven, I was studying at Harvard University. I was in the middle of preparing for my Ph.D. exams. It was a terribly arduous process and the homework scarcely allowed me time to breathe; I had no free time for anything outside of school. On occasion, I would learn something of what was happening in the world. I knew that it was becoming extremely chaotic and people were agitated. Many professors and students had already left school, and nothing more was heard from them. Overnight, some students lost contact with their homelands and wept in the dormitory. Under those uncertain circumstances, the school authorities urged the foreign students to stick calmly to our schoolwork. At that time, the United States had not been affected. So it was in those chaotic times I passed my Ph.D. exams, after which I was offered a job as an assistant professor in the history department.

"The teaching load of an assistant professor was very light, more like a form of practice. As a result, I had more time to find out about what was happening outside. At that time, the world had reached a point from which there was no turning back. From the perspective of history—my field—the complete collapse of civilization was approaching. The world had gone mad; chaos, disaster, and mass hysteria reigned; over a hundred strange cults appeared overnight, and the streets were filled with people shouldering crosses and fanatical believers carrying religious images. And invariably in the middle of the night someone was heard shouting: 'The end of the world is upon us; the end of the world is upon us!' A single religious meeting would attract tens of thousands. The preachers, who beat their breasts and stamped their feet, would work them into a state of hysteria—many would immolate themselves and many would have themselves crucified. At the same time, hedonism became all the rage, attracting ever greater numbers of people. Soon licentiousness, immorality, and even incest had become widespread. As the world was on the brink of going to hell, I was conscripted by the Nanning Committee. They informed me that my homeland, the small island that had been named the Light of the Pacific, had been obliterated. I and a few other fortunate survivors were charged with the difficult task of rebuilding our homeland. We would all receive the technical training necessary for the reconstruction. A few days later, I reported to a place that was like a military base. Tens of thousands of my compatriots were already there—they were the cream of my people. Actually, they were the only ones with the wherewithal to flee the disaster area. In addition to diplomats and immigrants, there were overseas students, military officers, government officials, scientists, engineers, doctors, lawyers, professors, wealthy people, movie stars, and some sailors.

"Afterward, little by little, we were deported to our homeland. I was enlisted in the last group to be sent back. When I landed, there were already a number of crude and simple buildings on the island. The vanguard of the new society, filled with energy and hope, hastened between the cranes and the concrete pipes. The adherents to the new faith, filled with hope and religious fervor, buried themselves in a myriad of plans and charts. I was assigned to the dam construction and engineering section, which had nothing whatsoever to do with what I had studied. Like others at the time, I had no complaints—our minds were filled with our work, the rebuilding of our home. Actually, the world was still in the midst of a cataclysm; on this point, Winston is perhaps correct, but as far as we were concerned, the catastrophe had passed. The only thing that lay ahead of us was a series of challenges, nothing else."

The professor had scarcely taken a breath as he spoke and halted here, his cheeks red and throat parched; his age demanded calm. Xi De had listened intently and was totally unaware that it was completely dark outside.

"Then you are saying, Professor, that Winston's accusations regarding Max Kristen are quite plausible."

The professor picked up his teacup and sipped slowly. After a while, he replied:

"Quite plausible. In those days there were a number of opinions, some of which were preposterous in the extreme. Some people felt he was the devil incarnate; others thought he was Christ come again for the last judgment at the end of days. It was the opinion of several friends of mine—all internationally recognized scholars—that the dramatic change seemed to possess a kind of causality all its own; in other words, that there was a discernible plan behind it all. Explosions in the Northern Hemisphere followed immediately upon the heels of those in the Southern Hemisphere. It was plain that a series of explosions in one area would severely disrupt the ecological balance of the globe. But all we did was talk; no one actually set out to thoroughly investigate the situation. I was busily engaged in the construction of the first modern dam here. Although I was in no way an expert, I learned from my colleagues that the design of the dam represented a new page in history. The other construction projects were basically the same. In that way, I devoted twenty years to such construction projects. Only when the work on all the cities—one administrative center, the five industrial cities, and the three agricultural cities—was nearly completed did they think of me and my educational background. When I say 'they,' I mean the regional committee, 90 percent of whom had been dispatched by the Nanning headquarters. At that time, the population of the island had reached about one million. Many compatriots had returned from various parts of the world because the violent changes had nearly come to an end. The schools once again had students, and I resumed my teaching career, teaching history at the Central Academy. I soon discovered that the field of history was not taken very seriously. This was not simply a case of the students being unwilling to slightly open the gates of memory due to lingering shock or fear after the catastrophe; even the committee was intentionally neglecting it. At any rate, after a number of years, few students elected to study the subject. The students were fixated in an unprecedented way on their major courses, owing to the specific way they were taught and the equipment available to them. A number of new discoveries and creations had received the painstaking encouragement and promotion of the authorities: the smallest success in outer space was met with the most enthusiastic response from the people. However, at the beginning of this extreme specialization, a group of generalists got together and asked me to join them. But I refused. I did so because I understood the inevitability of evolution and knew that there was no stopping change. They organized an underground group and even acquired weapons and issued a slogan, 'Hoodwinking the masses through specialization.' Unfortunately, by that time, most people had lost interest in revolution, struggle, and debate. They were willing, however, to go see a sci-fi flick by the title of *The Magellan Nebula* or to recline in a massaging chair. No one was willing to hear speeches on topics like "regaining the spiritual life" and "people cannot become like bees." For this reason, the revolution was soon stamped out, and some people fled to the mountains. The committee didn't bother to go after the fish that had slipped through the net. Instead, they put all their efforts into hastening the development of the new society. Twenty years ago, when the Third Committee announced the success of the election, the world's ten regional committees were on track, and no one would ever threaten such a tight, scientific, and effective organization again."

As the professor finished speaking, the living room fell silent. For a long time, neither of them said a thing. Finally, the professor broke the silence.

"Xi De, let's eat."

After eating, Xi De said good-bye to the professor and returned to the Bureau of Resource Analysis dorm, his mind an utter blank. The professor had not given him any clear instructions, but he had given him the name of one person, a former student of his. Perhaps he would be able to tell Xi De something about that revolutionary organization that had appeared so fleetingly.

Xi De lay down on his bed and took a slip of paper from his pocket on which was written: "Du Qun, Electricity Allocator, Administrative Department, Third Industrial City."

12

Lin Xing drained the last drop of green wine and waited to feel its heat rise in his stomach. What a comfortable feeling! His belly felt warm, as if there were a warm hand massaging his innards, massaging his guts, toying with his brain, and finally making him issue an uncontrollable sigh of happiness, satisfaction, and lasciviousness.

Forcing himself to open his blurry eyes, Lin Xing saw Xi De seated in the corner. At this late hour, the bar was nearly empty.

"Oh, brother," he said, knocking over several chairs before falling across the table at which Xi De sat.

"How could you get so drunk?" asked Xi De, his brow furrowed.

A short while later, in Lin Xing's apartment, Xi De helped him to bed.

The room was a mess—things were scattered all over, and the walls were covered in many colors of paint; seeing a shaggy-haired android beauty lying in the bathtub momentarily startled Xi De.

In the bathroom, Xi De found a sponge and a bottle of peppermint spirits. He soaked the sponge and placed it on Lin Xing's forehead; when the scent of peppermint entered his nose, he sneezed.

"Oh!" Lin Xing moaned. "Thanks, Xi De."

"You just have a good rest," he said. "I'm going home now."

"Hang on, Xi De, don't you want to know why I drink this way?"

"I don't care. I don't want to interfere in other people's private lives."

"Stupid liquor!" Lin Xing slapped his head with force and propped himself up. "Have a seat, Xi De. I've been transferred."

"Transferred?"

"Damn, and I received a performance award last year, you know. My performance was a little off this year, so they transfer me."

"Who do you mean by 'they'?"

"Those guys in HR, who else?"

"Why are they doing it to you?"

"They have their doubts about my loyalty. Damn it." Lin Xing continued angrily, "Who doesn't complain at the bureau? It's always the same every day. We're not robots."

"A transfer will be good—a change of scenery."

"What do you know, Xi De? You ought to go and see the outside world."

"The outside world?"

"Just out of school, I was the same as you," he said, his anger fading and his voice taking on a normal tone once again. "I believed that there was nothing better than having everything arranged for you—work, life, the future. Everything was planned; all you had to do was step lightly and be happy. The outside world doesn't exist. The only thing that matters to you is the Bureau of Resource Analysis."

"Huh." *What's so bad about that?* thought Xi De.

Since returning from the professor's, Xi De had been pondering many things related to the new society. Lin Xing was wrong in thinking that he didn't understand anything about the outside world. From Winston's writing and the professor, he actually knew more than most people. At best, Lin Xing was only a dilettante. He was just a little more sensitive to job fatigue than most. Job fatigue was unavoidable, like a machine wearing out. But the new society had a readjustment scheme for just such a problem. In a month, he'd receive two weeks of vacation and be sent to a rest area. But aside from those who worked in the Bureau of Character Readjustment in the Ministry of Education, no one knew the exact whereabouts of the rest area. From his colleagues who had been on such vacations, Xi De had learned that it was a totally unexpected and stimulating itinerary—there was even the possibility of taking a cruise to the moon on a spaceship. The term "readjustment" was spot-on. Readjustment for high-ranking administrators also implied a reward of sorts. So what was the reason for Lin Xing's conclusion that "The outside world doesn't exist. The only thing that matters to you is the Bureau of Resource Analysis"?

"I tell you, I'm being transferred to an agricultural city, where I'll have to live with those dumb farmers."

"Farmers are not necessarily dumb," said Xi De. "My parents are farmers."

"Sorry," said Lin Xing.

"I think I ought to be going," said Xi De. "Have a good night's sleep."

As Xi De neared the door, Lin Xing again called for him to stop.

"I forgot to tell you why I drink so every day."

Xi De looked back at Lin Xing sitting on his bed.

"Not long ago, one of my classmates worked in the data office of the Bureau of Resource Protection. One day he had an accident and broke a leg and was hospitalized. Initially, there was someone to cover for him, but unfortunately he had to go away on business. It just so happened I had to visit his office on business. It was then that I discovered something disturbing: there was no one in the office, but the work was being dealt with better than usual because there was a computer there. It had been sent by the administrative office and was doing his job. That's one reason for my heavy drinking . . ."

Xi De stopped listening, closed the door behind him, and returned to his own room.

13

A few days later, Lin Xing left and his replacement arrived, transferred from the First Industrial City. His name was Ge Shu, and he was an Asian-European mix, a graduate of the Secondary Academy. He had been given the job due to outstanding performance. It was said that he had won the award for being the most effective employee in his work unit five years running. In the Ministry of Resources, there was a group of several of this sort who rose, skirting regular channels. Through either a sense of inferiority or jealousy, they formed a small clique and drank and had fun together. It was said that they even swapped their android companions.

Ge Shu's office was next to Xi De's. He was tall and thin and had hairy hands. He was overly formal with others and spoke flatteringly. His two young female assistants liked to spread gossip about him. They called him a hick behind his back and said that he made a huge fuss about the features in the apartment he had been assigned.

In the Bureau of Resource Analysis dining hall, Ge Shu always nodded to Xi De. One time, Ge Shu even pulled up a chair for him. This sort of toadying behavior made his co-workers look at him with surprise.

"What is this? It smells so delicious," said Ge Shu, heaving a sigh.

This made the young ladies at the next table titter.

"It's called Kada—it's a food from outer space. It contains the purest form of protein," explained Xi De.

"Oh!" exclaimed Ge Shu. "We don't have this where I come from."

The laugher grew louder this time. Ge Shu's face flushed red.

"Don't pay any attention to them," said Xi De. "They're mean to strangers."

After work, Xi De took him to visit the various offices of the Bureau of Resource Analysis, the commissary, the bar, the gym, and the movie theater. They also played a game of billiards in the pool hall, where Xi De discovered that Ge Shu's skills were exceptional. Ge Shu explained that in his previous work unit, the most popular form of entertainment was billiards. Then Xi De asked about the industrial city; Ge Shu was pleased to answer all his questions—he viewed Xi De as his protector—and assured Xi De that if he visited the industrial city on official business, his friends would see to it that he enjoyed himself to the fullest.

From then on, Ge Shu was a frequent visitor to Xi De's office. Sometimes he would ask some technical questions; other times he'd just chat, that is, until that group of "climbers" discovered him. Only then did they drift apart.

This was the start of Xi De's unintentional contact with the outside world. The appearance of Ge Shu gave him a more concrete idea of that world.

A week later, Xi De was called to the director's office of the Bureau of Resource Analysis.

The director's office was luxuriously appointed. Scenic photos changed constantly on the wall screens. Xi De stood in the reception room enjoying the picture of a waterfall.

"Xi De." One of the doors of the reception room opened automatically, and the director's chair slid forward on specially built tracks. "That's Niagara Falls."

"It's a beautiful place."

"But that's not where you're going on your vacation." The director was a ruddy-complexioned, middle-aged man, and obviously a graduate of the Central Academy on account of the shiny lapel pin he wore. "The orders for your vacation have come down—our official computers just received the orders from the Ministry of Education. Here, take it—it's your vacation orders."

Xi De opened his orders.

Situmare City, Brazil. Three days hence, 8:30, Central Airport.

Xi De gave the director an inquiring look.

"I've been there once before—it's better than Niagara Falls. Niagara Falls is a lower-level resort area. Xi De, this is your first vacation!"

Xi De nodded.

"Don't think about anything. Just go and have a good time for two weeks," said the director, laughing mysteriously. "Your performance has been good, and your friendly attitude toward Ge Shu is to be praised." He seemed to know everything.

Xi De watched as the director disappeared behind the wall, then left the reception room.

14

The flying machine sped toward the northern horizon. More than a dozen passengers were seated in the cylindrical cabin, including two officials from the Ministry of Coordination, a systems analyst from the Ministry of Industry, and a rather stern-looking individual dressed in the khaki uniform of a Ministry of Education employee. They all got off midway through the journey. The remaining eight passengers—six men and two women—were from various regional committee offices. All wore Central Academy lapel pins. For this reason, they immediately formed small groups upon boarding and struck up conversations.

Xi De sat next to a tall, gaunt man of about thirty years of age with brown hair and dark eyes, who wore lightweight gray traveling clothes. He was a programmer from the Ministry of Technological Development, and was at that very moment excitedly describing his first adventure in outer space travel to his two listeners.

"In a state of weightlessness, you will have a strange and mysterious, transcendental experience. You might suddenly recall something forgotten since childhood. As you float in the air, you will have the sensation of sinking into cotton batting a hundred meters thick. You sink and sink and sink, until you no longer feel the need to worry about hitting something or breaking a leg. Thus, when you regain your cool, you relax your four limbs, then you close your eyes and sense the emptiness around you; your brain is the same. After a while, a strange scene will come to mind. It was then that I saw myself when I was a year old. . . ."

His listeners had increased. They sat in swivel seats that could turn a hundred and eighty degrees, allowing them to turn and face the space traveler.

"How did you get up there?" asked an attractive woman, who was around thirty.

"I went to the space station on official business for three weeks," replied the programmer proudly.

"Wow!" responded the woman, ogling him.

"Tell us what the space station was like," said another listener enthusiastically.

Xi De got up from his seat and walked over to the cockpit. He figured the guy was bragging and had probably done nothing more than visit a space module.

The pilot was a young black man. He turned and looked at Xi De and smiled. Xi De walked up behind him and looked out at the sky through the window.

The flying machine entered a cloudbank. The clouds parted as rapidly as fog.

"Situmare is beneath the clouds," said the pilot.

When the flying machine arrived on the runway at the Situmare Airport, a red tour bus designated as belonging to the Ministry of Education was already waiting.

Xi De and his fellow passengers all boarded the bus one by one. A ministry official shook hands with each of them, then in a loud voice announced:

"Welcome to Situmare, everyone!" His eyes swept over the anxiously expectant faces. "I'll be your host in the Situmare Recreation Zone. You can call me Callahan, and I'll be in charge of our trip from the airport to the recreation zone."

The bus sped over a spotless road. Glancing out the window, Callahan continued, "However, we are not allowed to stop or get off the bus in the downtown area. It's still a little way to the recreation zone."

No one asked anything; everyone understood the situation. One occasionally encountered the red buses from the Ministry of Education on the streets of Central City. The buses all had smoky glass windows and you couldn't see who was riding inside; nor was anyone ever seen getting off such buses.

After leaving the city, the bus entered a mountainous area. It stopped at a checkpoint between two steep cliffs. Two armed guards boarded the bus. One of them carried a small transmitter for checking the face of each passenger; the other one asked them each to hold out their hands so that he could check the ID numbers on the backs of their hands.

Everything was in order. The passengers took their luggage and got off the bus. After saying good-bye to Callahan and the driver, they walked through the checkpoint.

On the other side another tour bus was waiting. Upon boarding the bus, Xi De discovered that six strangers—two men and six women— were seated there. One blond woman with the face of an angel reached out and said to him:

"I am Zhen 143. You can call me Zhen; I'll be your guide."

"My name is Xi De," he replied, overwhelmed.

Never in his life had he seen such a lovely woman. Her eyes were as blue as water; she smiled with the easy familiarity of an old friend. The way she was dressed and made up also set Xi De's heart to thumping. After all, he was a normal young man. The two young ladies in the office couldn't compare to Zhen, though once in a while they appeared in his dreams. However, graduates of the Central Academy did possess more self-control that the average person. Although young people were allowed to court, such things were seldom encountered in the office. For this generation of young people, sex had been completely stripped of its mystery; sex possessed a purely biological function for them, the same as an appetite for food—when a person was hungry, they had to eat. The idea of love as the efflorescence of sex, a relic of the last century, was to them something akin to the civics class taken by primary school students. There was a time when a man and a woman might meet by chance on the street and, with a mutual glance, have a sexual fling and not be troubled in the least by morality or feelings. If you were willing, you could continue the relationship or be again like strangers the next day. By now people were disinclined. Sure, they needed it, but they didn't make a big deal about it. Sexual crimes were simply inconceivable.

Zhen was wearing a skin-tight silver tennis outfit, and her perky breasts, round bottom, and gorgeous pink legs made everyone gasp and gawk.

"I know you're Xi De," she said, snuggling up against him, the scent of roses assailing his nose. "I also know that you work at the Ministry of Resources in the 10th District, right?"

"Your information is very detailed." Zhen took his hand and placed it on her leg.

The bus proceeded along a beach lined with coconut palms. It was a beautiful summer scene of blue sky, beaches, waves, and sunlight. But no one on the bus paid the slightest attention—each was absorbed with the guide sitting next to them.

"I have to know something about you," Zhen replied coquettishly. "I have to know what you like to eat and drink, your hobbies, sleeping habits, and the things you like to talk about. Only then can I serve you well."

My goodness! Xi De cried to himself. *These women serve as more than just guides.* No wonder his colleagues always drifted off into bemused silence when they talked about their vacations.

"Based on my experience, I would say you have never been here before. Am I right?"

"This is my first vacation."

Who cares, said Xi De to himself, *there has to be a first time for everything*.

15

The Situmare Recreation Zone was set up specifically for the needs of high-ranking administrators. The zone, which covered a large area, supplied everything that was needed: all types of food, drink, and amusement; playing fields, swimming pools, beaches, and gardens. All the buildings were in the passionate, unrestrained Latin style. The walls were covered with brightly colored Indian motifs. Everywhere you looked were charmingly attired and happy couples: in the shade of enchanting trees, in dim coffee houses, and on intoxicating dance floors.

The vacationers arrived from the world's ten large regions and, despite the differences in hair color, skin, and facial features, they all expressed their shared feelings and joy as they lifted their glasses and sang of the world's glories using the same language.

In two short weeks, Xi De had fallen into a colorful and profligate dream world. He had experienced all forms of unimaginable sensual stimulation. In bed, Zhen used all of her charms to allow him to experience the ultimate pleasures of the flesh. After yet another unreal climax, Zhen told him of her lot. She was an orphan and from an early age had been educated in a special school. The school had used every means to transform her into an intoxicating blossom: every mechanical method had been utilized to perfect her body; drugs had been used to give her skin its honeyed sheen. She had taken specialized classes in sexual technique; the art of conversation; bearing; and the psychological responses of men. In addition, she had to learn to dance and sing. Finally, she was told that her ultimate goal in life was to please others, and in that way make herself happy. Her world was the recreation zone; the outside world held no interest for her. From the men she had entertained, she knew all about the outside, its regimentation, its boringness, the tragedy of a world in which people worked to survive and not to be happy. Of course she was not interested. She was happy and satisfied right where she was and she was willing to stay there the rest of her life.

Xi De narrowed his eyes as he quietly listened to Zhen's lovely voice. Her innocence and joy were totally sincere. With such feelings of gratitude, Zhen climbed out of bed and danced slowly and solemnly in the nude. She began to sing.

I am a rose in Heaven,
Beautiful and alluring, loved by all.
She is not sad or troubled,
Happiness is all she wants.
I am a happy rose in Heaven
A rose with no worries, praised by all.
She has no past and no future,
Now is all she has.

Love me one and all, love this joyful rose,
Let her happy laughter fill your world,
Let her song accompany you through interminable night. . . .

And Xi De slipped into a dream listening to her luscious, happy song.

The following day, Zhen escorted him to see some special places in the recreation zone; they were different from other eating and drinking establishments and were hard to get into. They squeezed in among the emotional crowd in a building that resembled the Roman Colosseum and watched a man battle a lion, gorging on the bloody feast.

"Kill it! Kill it! You bastard . . ."

"Kill! Kill! Make mincemeat out of it . . ."

"Stab it! Stab it again! Make mincemeat out of it . . ."

The air was filled with piercing screams, shouts, and the sound of gnashing teeth. Zhen's hands were clenched in tight fists; she half squatted and half sat in her seat; her eyes looked as if they would pop out of her head as she fixed them on the arena. In addition to screaming incessantly, the black-haired beauty sitting next to her tore continuously at her own hair.

In such an infectious atmosphere, Xi De couldn't help but shout as well.

The arena was total confusion, the ground covered with blood. Bodies ripped apart by the lion lay scattered in pieces all around. Without a doubt the lion was victorious as it lowered its head to gnaw on a femur; the circular motion of its lower jaw never ceased, making it look like a child with a lollipop. The spectators in the stands stopped shouting; they cursed as they hurled their beverage bottles into the arena.

Xi De left the arena with Zhen, but before they had gone very far, Zhen pulled him down a nearby street into a flower garden.

"I can hardly wait," said Zhen, panting. That bloody scene had left her extremely excited.

"But there are people here."

"Who cares?" Zhen hurriedly stripped off her pants and lay down on the ground. "Come on, Xi De, come on . . ."

After they had finally grown still and lay entwined in the grass and bushes, they heard shouts from nearby.

They couldn't help but look at each other and laugh.

"There are quite a few people hidden away in here," said Zhen.

"Who were those guys who got eaten by the lion?" asked Xi De.

"They are the half-witted descendants of those exposed to radiation."

"What do you mean by exposed to radiation?"

"You don't know?"

"Those infected by radioactivity?"

"More or less. But these people are their descendants. They have low IQs, are physically deformed, and are ugly beyond belief," said Zhen, "and like the animals, they are raised in the caves behind us."

"Are visitors allowed?"

"Who'd want to see such disgusting things?"

In the days that followed, they visited similar locations, a casino and a sexual paradise. In the latter, they observed exhibitions of all sorts of unusual and perverted sexual games: bestiality, homosexual intercourse, and all sorts of unbelievable sadistic sexual practices.

In the evening there was an orgy with many people exchanging partners and engaging in all sorts of group sex. Xi De refused several invitations, which made Zhen happy. When it came time to say good-bye, Zhen gave Xi De a small gift: a small silver idol.

"This is a very old religious talisman. How did you come to possess such a thing?"

"Someone gave it to me."

"Oh. Thank you," he said in a heartfelt manner. "I'll miss you."

"No," she said shaking her head. "We'll never meet again. You'd best not think of me."

She helped him pin on the silver idol.

"It'll protect you," she said gaily. "Good-bye, Xi De!"

16

After returning to work, Xi De became more reticent. Zhen now occupied an important place in his heart. He would often think of her at night, and when he did his heart would feel a slight pain. It was only a six-hour flight to Situmare; in just six hours he could hold her in his arms. But he also knew that it was just wishful thinking on his part and that he would never see her again for the rest of his life. Not only did a wall of distance separate them; the entire system, the institutions and organizations of the new society were set as insurmountable obstacles against them. Lin Xing and many others perhaps had had similar experiences. Sometimes he felt he could detect a fleeting expression on the faces of his colleagues that seemed to indicate that they, like him, felt that something was wrong. Was it the whole social system? Or was it the lack of maturity in an individual mind?

He had been a member of the new society for about two years now. In that time, he had had a good many inexplicable experiences of which others had no inkling. Worse yet, the influence of the professor and Winston had been pronounced, providing him with a degree of self-consciousness well beyond the average. He couldn't in good conscience use the clear, simple logic of the new society to manage his daily life. Unlike others, he was incapable of rationalizing the feelings he had for Zhen. If Zhen was like the analytical apparatus in the branch office of the Bureau of Resource Analysis, she was painstakingly designed to revitalize your character so that you could continue with your work. Both man and machine had to be restored, because there was nothing in the world that could be guaranteed to function forever. This being the case, Zhen was your lubricant; otherwise, she was just a living android beauty. You needed her the way you needed food, sleep, and amusement. If you developed feelings for her, then those feelings still originated in necessity and not in something irrational. Every person was an independent entity that had to fulfill their own needs; the so-called "union of souls" was nothing more than a useless, abstract concept. Union? Nothing was more independent or complete than the soul. Then how were two souls supposed to achieve union? If he thought of her now and longed to be with her, it was because she satisfied the needs of body and soul. Through her skills, he had achieved previously unknown sensual satisfaction; the sight of her beauty filled him with incomparable joy; her tenderness relieved him of all forms of anxiety. But what of her soul? Did she know what love was? Did her vocabulary contain the word "soul"?

Xi De tossed and turned in bed. He wished that someone could answer these vague metaphysical questions. Strictly speaking, his intellectual education was nothing more than a professional technical education. In school, no one had the slightest opportunity to come in contact with knowledge beyond their studies. The knowledge required for one field was sufficient to keep one occupied for life. Who had time to discuss things such as the meaning of life, how to live, values, and other such abstract concepts of no practical use? In fact, the new society was a whole that was designed through strict planning, scientific analysis, and the computer. The way you lived life and your values were defined by society; the slightest deviation from the normal course would certainly result in harm. There was an old slogan to explain this kind of situation: "Freedom is simply not hampering the freedom of others." This slogan revealed the mysteries of the new society and the error of people in the past. Actually, there wasn't a single form of freedom that didn't hamper others.

Now I have doubts about the definition of man, thought Xi De. *When I do, I have already hampered society in its definition of man and thereby have harmed others.* The ancients defined man as a being who exists for the sake of seeking the meaning of life, but it was different in the new society, "in which each person is a cog in the machine that operates perpetually; and a cog cannot conceive of itself as anything other than a cog." The quote was from a book, and it sounded reasonable. *If I ask myself why I exist, there could be a thousand answers, not one of which is right. In the past, a person could exist for his god, for an ideal, or even purely for the sake of existence. Today, however, religion has been debunked, and no ideal can surpass the perfection of "the establishment of an eternal human paradise"; such an ideal could in no way be considered Platonic. And what conceptualization of a human paradise in the history of humankind could be more perfect than that of the new society?*

Xi De rolled over. Feeling a hard, metallic object under his neck made him break off his crazy thoughts. It was that small silver idol on a chain.

He lifted it and stroked the idol and thought of the word "Christian." The old history professor had once mentioned the religion in class, saying that it had had the greatest influence of any religion in the history of human civilization. At its zenith, it counted half of the world's population among its faithful. It was hard to believe that humanity could worship something so amorphous. And even so, Christianity was unable to relieve the afflictions of humankind. By the end of the twentieth century and the commencement of the third industrial revolution, its partial opposition to science and progress were its downfall.

I can't think about this anymore. Xi De got out of bed and poured himself a glass of water. It was already two in the morning. He stood spacing out for a while in front of the clock. Then, under a sudden impulse, he dressed, opened the door, and stepped out into the quiet hall and its gentle light. He continued on past tightly shut doors to the elevator, where he pushed the button.

Xi De saw his face in the elevator mirror. It was a pale, haggard face, hair disheveled, eyes dull and empty, like those of a drunkard returning from a bar. But the bar was closed, as were all the other entertainment establishments in the building. Perhaps he could leave the building and go to some other street to find the same sort of place.

The elevator door opened and Xi De walked toward the main entrance, his footsteps resounding against the shiny floor. Seeing himself reflected in the metallic wall gave him the sensation that someone was watching and waiting in the corner. He quickened his pace and left the Resource Building.

It was a crisp autumn evening with a slight breeze. Both hands thrust in his pockets, Xi De looked ahead at the empty street. In the bluish light of the street lamps, the skyscrapers in the shadows became dark and menacing. Xi De lacked the courage to cross the avenue, which was broad enough for twenty cars to drive side by side. So instead, he continued down the sidewalk with no destination in mind.

At an intersection, a police car pulled up and stopped beside him. A policeman stepped out of the car and in an amiable manner asked:

"Sir, what are you doing walking alone here so late at night?"

"I couldn't sleep."

"Can I check your ID?"

Xi De stretched out his hand.

"AH5481," the policeman said to the other. He turned to Xi De and saluted.

"I'm sorry, but this is standard procedure."

In a few minutes, the policeman in the car said, "Everything is in order with AH5481."

After having been hassled, Xi De felt his mind clearer as the police car drove away. He continued on until he found himself standing beside a canal.

Sitting on the embankment, he gazed at the stars twinkling on the water's surface.

As the days passed, Xi De developed a habit of going for a walk at midnight. Several days a week he would sit on the embankment for an hour or two, mulling over complicated issues.

Finally, one day the director summoned him to his office.

"Xi De, over the last two or three months, we have discovered that you cannot keep your mind on your work," said the director, examining him.

"I'm sorry, Director, but I have been troubled by a number of things recently."

"I have found myself in the same situation. Furthermore, I believe that anyone who returns from their first vacation is bound to be a bit absentminded. This is to be expected and tolerated. But we have noticed that your absentmindedness has extended well beyond a week and has lasted three months now."

"I know, but . . ."

"In principle, we allow the individual to work things out in his own way in such cases. We refer to this as a transitional period in the maturation of character. But your case is beyond the norm, so we have no choice but to help you." The director paused, heaved a sigh, and said, "The computer indicates that a change of work environment is in order for you."

17

The Third Industrial City was situated beside a lake in the central part of the island and was under the jurisdiction of the Industrial Board of the Tenth Regional Committee. The city had a population of two hundred thousand and produced mainly textiles, steel, and plastics, and had several other kinds of light industry.

The City Administrative Building was twenty stories tall and stood facing the enchanting lake. Xi De's office was on the twelfth floor. It was a branch office of the Resource Analysis Bureau with only a dozen or so employees. The principal work of the office was to collect the production statistics from every industry in the city, do the preliminary review, and then send them to headquarters in Central City.

Xi De was the only employee in the branch office who was a graduate of the Central Superior Academy. On account of this, his colleagues were eventually able to accept this taciturn young man who seemed to be wrapped up in his own thoughts all day long.

The difference between Xi De's office and that of headquarters was like night and day: there were no young female assistants, no coffee, no automatically adjusting color walls. Even the work computers seemed lifeless. Fortunately, his office window looked out on an inexhaustible beauty of lake and mountains. Most of the time, Xi De stood at his window, staring blankly at the scenery. With his high-level training, the tasks in the branch office were easy to perform. Soon, several colleagues came to consult with him on a number of small professional matters. Xi De's patience and smile quickly earned him their friendship. For those from the secondary academies in a branch that couldn't compare with Central City, the greatest success in life was to work at headquarters. The dissatisfaction and fatigue that resulted from the boring work and the scorn and hostility among high-level managers were rarely encountered here. Xi De's arrival no doubt left them stunned. For this reason, both sides were initially at a loss. Even the chief of the branch, normally such a jovial heavy-set person, watched every move he made with great suspicion.

One day, the stout fellow appeared at Xi De's office.

"Xi De," he said, cautiously observing Xi De's expression. When he finally realized he harbored not the slightest hostility, he relaxed a bit. "We're having drinks at my house this evening. You're welcome to join us."

"Thank you, Chief," Xi De replied warmly. "I'll be there."

That night at the cocktail party was the first time Xi De became aware of the lively, straightforward lifestyle in the city. He observed everything going on around him with a good deal of curiosity: unbridled conversation, casual attire, flowing spirits, shouting, and rivalries for women. The stout chief brought a stunning woman over to Xi De.

"Allow me to introduce you. This is Lian Lian; she works in statistics. Lian Lian, this is Xi De, a graduate of the Central Superior Academy."

"Wow!" replied Lian Lian, startled. "That's really something."

They departed together after the cocktail party ended.

"I live in the singles dorm of the Bureau of Statistics," said Lian Lian, pointing ahead. "It's a ten-minute walk in that direction."

Other than the occasional passing police car, not another car was seen on the street. All administrative dorms were concentrated within a twenty-minute walk.

"You're alone?"

"I have no parents," she replied. "They worked at the hydrogen plant in the Second Industrial City, but they were killed in an accident. What about you?"

"My parents live in an agricultural city."

After a short distance, Lian Lian took his hand and sat with him on an iron bench beside the road.

"It's a beautiful night," she said. "There are quite a few people out for strolls."

Xi De grew quiet. This place was totally unlike Central City, which was so cold and forbidding. Couples and groups of chatting young people sat under the bright streetlights. There was scarcely ever anyone on the streets of Central City after dark; everyone was busy with their own affairs in their own little spaces. The night's activities were on the television screens courtesy of Central Television: all you had to do was get comfortable on the sofa and you could participate in any sort of game or televised discussion. If you felt like taking a break or drinking, the rooftop garden or ground-floor bar could be reached by elevator. But here, owing to a lack of electronic equipment, most people spent their time with other people.

"Xi De, can I ask you something?"

"Go ahead."

"How did you end up here?"

"I had some problems with my job efficiency."

Xi De's frankness left her a bit embarrassed.

"I've never been to Central City, but I hear that it's paradise."

"Perhaps." Xi De shrugged his shoulders.

"I hear you can get anything you want there," she added.

This time, Xi De did not answer. They stood up and headed toward Lian Lian's place.

It was a square, orderly apartment complex. At the door, she asked:

"Would you like to come up and sit a while?"

"Thanks," said Xi De, "but it's late."

It was a month before Xi De received another invitation from her. That night he slept with her.

"Xi De, am I good?" asked Lian Lian, lying next to him.

"Yes," replied Xi De gloomily. A moment before he had been thinking about Zhen in Situmare.

"Compared with the girls of Central City?"

"I don't know."

"I don't believe you," said Lian Lian, becoming pettish. "I don't believe you, I don't believe you."

"Really, I don't know."

"I hear the girls there are like snakes and they take drugs."

"Says who?"

"The people in my office. They say that high-ranking cadres have access to aphrodisiacs."

"How do they know?"

"They heard it from other people."

Xi De was somewhat surprised. There were so many rumors about Central City here. Many of his co-workers had asked him about them but had always been skeptical about his answers. The cadres in industrial cities were only allowed to visit Central City on official business. It was difficult to get permission to visit family there.

"They said you were sent here as punishment for some offense and that sooner or later you'll be sent back. Right?"

"I don't know."

"I'd really like to go to Central City."

"Why?"

"I'm bored here," sighed Lian Lian, turning her naked back to Xi De. "It's always the same old thing; I really want to get out of here. . . ."

18

Three months passed before Xi De was allowed to leave the Administrative District and go to the Steel Factory District due to computer problems there. The memory had become corrupted, and he was ordered to go and oversee repairs.

At the entrance to the factory district, Xi De showed his pass. Then he was escorted to the security office, where a middle-aged man in blue work clothes was waiting for him.

"Hello, Mr. Xi. I am the assistant director of the production statistics office. Welcome."

They took their seats in a small electric cart.

"Security here is very strict," observed Xi De.

"Something happened recently," replied the assistant director.

Xi De didn't pursue the matter. The cart passed among a number of tall buildings, from some of which ear-splitting banging was heard, from some of which fiery light was seen.

The cart slowed in front of a burned-out building where a group of people were gesticulating.

"Look at that," said the assistant director. "They've been at it again."

"Who?"

"The Defend the Earth Army."

"Defend the Earth Army," Xi De said, astonished. "What's that?"

"You've never heard of them?" he asked incredulously. "How can you people in administration not know?"

"I'm new here."

"No wonder. The Defend the Earth Army is probably composed of a bunch of workers with mental problems. Their favorite thing to do is burn down buildings. At least they don't hurt people."

"Why did they choose such a strange name?"

"Who knows?"

At a building covered in gray sheet metal, they got out of the cart.

"They'll never be able to burn this building," said the assistant director in the elevator.

When the elevator door opened, they stepped into the statistics office.

It was a big, bustling office, with many people moving to and fro; the walls were covered with charts and graphs. Instruments for analysis, fax machines, and computers were everywhere. Each and every machine emitted its own sound. The air was filled with an atmosphere of anxiety and efficiency. A woman stood up from a table where an electric typewriter sat—she was the assistant to the assistant director. She proceeded to lead the way.

Three or four people were standing around the computer that was having problems.

"The guy from administration is here," said the assistant director. "How's it coming?"

"More than one place has been corrupted," replied one of them, without lifting his head.

"Before the office closes," said the assistant director, "I'll contact administration and ask them to let you stay another day. You can sleep at my place."

Dusk fell quickly. With the others getting off work, they left the statistics office.

"The residential district is next to the factory. It's only a ten-minute walk from here," said the assistant director. "You'd better not show that pass so as to avoid trouble with security."

The residential district hugged the shore of the lake, and by the light of the setting sun the buildings cast long reflections on the lake's surface.

"Our residences can't compare with those in the Administrative District, but our houses, which are made out of synthetic materials, have their good points—they look a little more alive."

On both sides of the wide street stood neat rows of colorful two-story houses, each with a small lawn and a few bushes in front.

"There are several thousand residences here in the Factory District," said the assistant director. "Everyone is allocated a house, but the higher your position, the bigger the house and the better the facilities."

"These two-story houses look plenty comfortable," commented Xi De. "Sometimes I don't like to take the elevator."

"We're almost there. It's still early. Let's go get a drink first."

"Do you live alone?"

"No. I have a wife. We've been married for twenty years. She works in the commissary."

"Do you have any kids?"

"No. We've never been authorized."

They chatted as they walked. The street was full of people who had just gotten off work. Some, arms around each other's shoulders, sang.

A pretty girl approached from the opposite direction. They both fixed their eyes on her at the same time.

"It'll be even livelier later; just wait and see," said the assistant director. "Ah, here's the bar."

The bar was filled with workers just off work. The assistant director frowned and pushed his way toward the bar with Xi De.

"My wife and I really hope to live in the Administrative District," said the assistant director, raising a glass.

Xi De took a sip. It was a bitter, low-quality wine.

"Is there any green liquor?"

"Goodness!" said the assistant director. "I've only had that a few times in my life, and that was at the factory director's house."

"What are those people doing?"

"They're playing computer games. Lousy punks, I can't stand 'em. Let's finish our drinks and get out of here."

As they were leaving, a worker started singing that popular song in a loud voice:

There is no past, there is no future,
There is nothing but the present for us.
There is no sadness, there is no happiness,
There is nothing but indifference for us.

There is no argument, there is no splitting,
There is nothing but work for us.

At the assistant director's lovely acrylic table, Xi De sat chewing a steak. "The steak is from New Zealand. Have some more," said the hostess in all politeness. She was a plump, middle-aged woman with small eyes.

"Hemei is very happy," said the host. "We so rarely have the opportunity to entertain a guest from the Administrative District."

After dinner, his host took Xi De out. His wife begged off, claiming a headache.

Night had already fallen, but the streets were lit as bright as day as people came and went. Filled with curiosity, Xi De stared wide-eyed, taking in everything around him.

To him, the lives of the lowest stratum of people in the new society were so true that they seemed almost unreal. Although he had seen snippets from news broadcasts on television about a celebration or something, he had never seen life firsthand for himself. The impression was quite different—the infectious excitement, the hubbub or an unexpected shout, seemed to have a physicality all their own that struck you, willing or not.

"These people don't know how to use their heads," said the assistant director, dodging a young fellow who tried to butt him with his shoulder. "All they know how to do is cause trouble."

"Do they just roam the streets when they get off work?"

"Yes! What else are they supposed to do?"

This made sense to Xi De. The life of a worker had been so simplified that it consisted of only two important parts (the life of a farmer was a different story).

The first part consisted of professional training. As children, they had been assigned by the Ministry of Education to study at one of the many vocational schools until they grew up. These schools imparted a single, limited curriculum; the training received by the students amounted to nothing more than the continuing of a technical skill. For a newly graduated electrician from one of these schools, a comprehensive knowledge of all the electronic devices in the new world was sufficient to occupy him for a lifetime. Of course, there was no way to acquire the knowledge of any other field, if he had the will to do so. The second part consisted of private life after work. The most important thing here was the indulgence of one's instincts. The workers could amuse themselves in satisfying their desires and hopes in a richly varied material life. As to spiritual life, the workers lacked the basic concepts and vocabulary to be aware of their emptiness. They were allowed to paint and perform music, but they were limited to the simple smearing of pigments and strumming an instrument. The workers could not partake of a higher artistic realm, nor did they have the least interest in doing so.

Xi De and his host stood listening to a street performance. The four musicians played simple quartets. The many spectators applauded at each pause in the music.

"Their greatest hope is to be able to perform on television in Central City," said the assistant director to Xi De. "We hold a musical competition every year."

"Do they write their own songs?"

"No, the music is distributed by the Ministry of Education."

As they exited the crowd, several people eyed the pass on Xi De's lapel with curiosity, but that was as far as it went. They entered another bar for a drink and played a pinball-like computer game, but because of Xi De's lack of skill, they only played half a game, the assistant director finding it boring.

"Let's go someplace else," said the assistant director, already a bit tipsy. "You have to experience everything to the fullest."

"What sort of place?"

"It's a high-class place, a real high-class place."

As they turned down a different street, a huge neon sign suddenly appeared before them.

"Ke Ke's Bar?"

"Ke Ke is the name of the owner. He is one of the wealthy people here."

Xi De found the word "wealthy" very strange. Perhaps only such a place produced such people. In Central City, money conferred very little special power. And after the elimination of the currency system, the most a person could buy with it were articles of daily use, none of which would be lacking to a high-ranking administrator.

"Wealthy?" he couldn't help but ask.

"The guy has more money than you can shake a stick at. His house is fixed up like a palace, and he always has five or six mistresses."

"How'd he get so much money?"

"By opening bars and casinos, among other things."

"Oh." So such places still existed in the Industrial District.

It was a luxurious bar with thick carpet. Next to the bar was a small dance floor on which several women in hot pants were bumping and grinding. They found a seat near the dance floor. The assistant director tossed a small copper onto the floor and the girls twisted even more vigorously.

"Tart," he muttered.

"Why are you still using money here?"

"Can you gamble without it?" asked the assistant director. "The committee had to okay it, but only in the Factory District and not in the Administrative District."

At that moment a heavy-set fellow in a bright red shirt approached. His laughter could be heard at some distance.

"Assistant Director, you haven't forgotten me, have you?

"Nonsense, Ke Ke. This is Xi De from the Administrative District."

"A rare visitor, a rare visitor," said the portly fellow, stretching out his hand. "Welcome."

He sat down as he spoke.

"Brother Xi, in which department do you work?"

"Don't be scheming now," said the assistant director.

"I work in resource analysis."

"That's a good place. I have some friends in the commodities section," said Ke Ke. "Jin Qi, Li Shilin . . ."

"I don't know them," replied Xi De. "I haven't been in the Administrative District long."

"That's okay," said Ke Ke, a bit disappointed, "that's okay."

"Ke Ke," said the assistant director, "this is Mr. Xi's first visit here. What have you got to show him?"

"You needn't say more," said the portly fellow. "Let's go to the box."

The curtain to the box moved and Ke Ke entered, holding a bottle of wine, with two women in revealing dress.

"This is Qing Qing, this is Lu Lu, and this is a bottle of red liquor I got from the Administrative District," he said. "I have some business to attend to so I can't stay."

After Ke Ke left, the box became quite boisterous. At first Xi De was at a loss, but he soon came around.

"Assistant Director," said Xi De, "how did he get his hands on a bottle of this?"

"He is very resourceful and can bring things in from the Administrative District," said the assistant director, holding Lu Lu. "Don't worry about it, Xi De. Let's drink. Lu Lu, offer him a toast."

After half a round they became aware of a disturbance on the other side of the curtain, following which the curtain parted and a drunk and angry young man forced his way in. Ke Ke hurriedly rushed in to block him.

"Oh! So here you are."

"We can talk things over, Xu," said the stout fellow, becoming somewhat anxious.

"So it's you," said Xu, looking at the man sitting next to Lu Lu. "Assistant Director, what a pal!"

"We can talk things over, we can talk things over, we're all friends here," Ke Ke kept repeating.

"Who is he?" Xi De couldn't help but ask.

"He's an officer from the police affairs section," said the assistant director, frowning, "and he's drunk. What a pain!"

The police officer continued to cause a scene for a while before deciding to focus his attention on one of the young ladies right before him. He reached to grab Qing Qing, who was behind Xi De.

"What are you doing?" asked Xi De, preventing him.

"Who are you?" The police officer seemed to sober up and paused before pressing his face close to Xi De.

"He is an official from the Administrative District," interjected Ke Ke.

"I don't care what district he's from. This is the Factory District, not the Administrative District," he said, steeling his heart. "Hold out your hand, I want to check your ID."

"He *is* from the Administrative District," said the assistant director, becoming angry. "You must not have noticed his pass. There is a limit to such jokes."

"I don't care. Hold out your hand. I don't trust passes."

He's raising hell just to raise hell, thought Xi De. He did stretch out his hand and place it before the young man's eyes.

"AH5481," read the police officer. By the time he reached the last number, he was entirely sober.

"Good Lord!" shouted the stout fellow.

"A . . ." muttered the police officer, frightened. "You're a central official?"

Silent, Xi De stood up. He never expected that the ID number on the back of his hand could have such an impact here.

"It's okay. There's been a mistake," said the assistant director, patting the police officer on the shoulder, all smiles. "Old Xu, I told you that you had too much to drink, but you wouldn't listen to me. Hurry up and apologize to his honor."

The police officer stood stunned for a while before stammering:

"S-sorry, S-sir . . ."

"Forget it."

A profoundly unfathomable smile appeared on Xi De's face.

19

The following day, Xi De said good-bye to the assistant director and his wife, boarded a boat, crossed the lake, which was mirror-smooth, and returned to the Administrative District on the opposite shore. He stopped by the office, exchanged a few words with his colleagues, and then returned to the dormitory.

It was a row of five-story buildings closely neighboring the administrative buildings. He lived on the fourth floor and could see a corner of the lake from his window, as well as the swimming pool and tennis court below. There was no one in the swimming pool at the moment; a life preserver floated on the blue water. Similarly, the tennis court was empty save for someone apparently repairing the net. Xi De's gaze rested on the man for a moment. Stepping away from the window, he took off his jacket. It was a bright spring morning and his room was a little stuffy. He turned on the air conditioner, opened the refrigerator, and poured himself a glass of juice. He sat down on the sofa to quietly wait for dusk to arrive.

People in the Administrative District got off work at three, by which time the public facilities would be crowded, the sound of laughter echoing amid the horseshoe-shaped buildings and floating in through his window.

Xi De shifted his position on the couch till he was almost horizontal. His head still ached from the revelries of the previous night. What was the Factory District really like? What kind of people really lived there? He thought of stout Ke Ke, the police officer, the dancing girls, and the street musicians and wondered what they were really doing. They were certainly not the well-behaved, obedient citizens who arrived at work on time like in books or as reported by the Central News. They fought, schemed, gambled, and engaged in shady business. Perhaps that was what Lin Xing meant by "the world outside." He wondered how Lin Xing was doing. Then he thought of Zhen and his previous pain began to subside. Time was a strange thing. Zhen had gradually receded behind the gauze curtain of a dream and now, standing on this side of the curtain, he saw a whole, sharply different world appear before him. He was no longer that docile, knock-kneed graduate of Central Academy sitting at his desk, but rather a mature and worldly adult. More precisely, he had begun to understand the world outside of textbooks and television. But what was the nature of his understanding?

Xi De lay down on the couch and closed his eyes. At that moment, he heard the sound of young people shouting outside. A few minutes later the shouts rose one after another, mixed with the sound of people diving into water.

Xi De continued his train of thought. According to the description in the first chapter of his civics textbook, the new society was the most advanced and perfect society in the history of human civilization. In this society, everyone received the education best suited to their IQ and disposition and was given the fairest and most reasonable opportunities for work. At the same time, they also enjoyed sufficient material reward and hopes for promotion permitted by their class. Administrators in Central City, for example, had the best work environment, the most reasonable work hours, the material comforts befitting their status, and an annual vacation to blow off any excess energy. In the industrial cities, the material comforts were the same; the difference was the quality. Of course, that difference was an effective stimulus for the lower classes to improve themselves. But what about in terms of the spirit? The new society did not necessarily discount the importance of spiritual satisfaction, but it did reject all abstract metaphysical notions. But in point of fact, most metaphysical notions were constructed out of a bunch of vague and obscure terms. Religion was a good example. If a deity could appear before men, then the new society would allow you your religious faith. But in thousands of years, no god had appeared outside the pages of a book, and not one of the books had been written by anyone other than ordinary, opinionated human beings. Therefore it was plain to see that spiritual satisfaction was not something transcendental, but could be obtained from love, marriage, appetite, sex, or human relationships.

Although this was the case, why was it that the workers in the Industrial District could not find satisfaction within the order of the new society and continued to cling to the immaturity of humanity in the last century?

An answer began to take shape for Xi De.

"It was the basic nature of humanity." This answer came like a shock. A perfect environment could not eliminate humanity's innate flaws: greed, swindling, risk taking, and degeneration. Why? Why?

The sound of the doorbell brought him back to himself. It was Lian Lian. Glowing with health, she was wearing a pair of shorts that revealed her long, healthy legs.

"What are you up to, Xi De?"

"I was just thinking."

"What's there to think about? Come on, let's go swimming."

"I'm not feeling well."

"Well," said Lian Lian, becoming unhappy, "one trip to the Industrial District and you end up like this."

"Have you ever been there?"

"No way, but I've heard all about that rotten place."

Rotten. That was the word! Lian Lian was right. The most perfect things were the most likely to become rotten.

In half a century, as the world was approaching perfection, it had perhaps already started to rot at the roots.

"Okay, Lian Lian, let's go swimming."

When they got out of the swimming pool, his girlfriend said to him: "A friend of mine at the Electric Power Agency is having a cocktail party tonight. What do you say we go?"

There was an endless series of small cocktail parties in the Administrative District; Xi De was already well accustomed to them. In Central City, such face-to-face encounters among people were no longer popular. Using the latest information technology, they could take part in all sorts of activities via the screens in their own living rooms. Xi De had once been a judge on a television game show without even knowing where the competition was held.

"If you like," said Xi De.

It was a small party held by one of her girlfriends in the dorm. There were only eleven or twelve couples invited. After eating, they danced. Lian Lian seemed especially excited, her laughter resounding. A young man asked her to dance. She glanced at Xi De and he nodded and then sat in the corner to watch the men and women dancing in the living room.

"She's a real live wire," said a middle-aged man sitting next to him.

Xi De turned and politely smiled.

"My name is Du Qun," said the middle-aged man. "I work at the power distribution section."

"I'm Xi De." They shook hands. "I've heard of you someplace."

"That's impossible," said the middle-aged man, looking somewhat startled.

"Let me think," said Xi De, racking his brain. "Right, it was from Professor Kang Zaoshi."

20

Not long after the party, they ran into each other again at a regatta. It was a bright and clear Sunday. A large viewing stand had been erected on the shore of the lake between the Administrative District and the Factory District. High-spirited city residents were crowded in the shade of the trees and canopies. It was the annual regatta held by the Third Industrial City. Xi De sat with the officials from the Administrative District, watching with pleasure the opening ceremonies. The opening remarks were given by the head of administration, followed by remarks by high-ranking officials of Central City, including the head of the Department of Recreation in the Ministry of Education as well as several officials from the Ministry of Domestic Affairs. The regatta began after the speeches concluded. Colorful sailboats filled the lake amid the general uproar as the spectators swarmed along the shore. A number of those sitting next to Xi De leaped off the viewing stand. Soon only Xi De and several older officials remained.

"Aren't you going to go down to the lake and cheer?" asked Du Qun, suddenly appearing beside him.

"Oh, it's you, Mr. Du," said Xi De, shaking hands with him. "I'm not one for noisy crowds."

"The same here," he said. "Who do you think will win?"

"I don't know. What do you think?"

"Last year the textile factory won. This year it's hard to predict."

There was a moment of silence. Xi De looked toward the lake, but vaguely felt Du looking at him from the side.

"Xi De," the voice sounded as if it were coming from another world, "why were you sent to Industrial City?"

"What?"

"Nothing," the voice said, returning to normal. "It's strange. Central officials are rarely ever transferred to a lower level."

"My performance was poor."

Such a frank reply left Du Qun flustered.

"Before me, my colleague Lin Xing was transferred to an agricultural city."

"Lin Xing. I've heard his name. His father was an interstellar spaceship commander."

"Interstellar ship?"

"But his ship vanished year before last."

"Oh." *That explains things,* thought Xi De. "Why did it vanish? Did they ever find out why?"

"I don't know," he said, shaking his head. "There are a lot of things we don't need to know."

After that, Du often visited Xi De at his place. They talked about things at the academy and in Central City. Sometimes they spent all night talking. Xi De strangely felt that Du was trying to probe his innermost thoughts. Du took great pains to find out everything about his relationship with the old professor. Du told Xi De that he had looked at the old professor's antiques and had listened to him talk about history, but he felt that the professor harbored many secrets he would never tell anyone else. On this point, Xi De smiled and said nothing.

One evening, Du Qun told him his own life story:

"My parents, like yours, were both farmers, but they died early. At six I entered the Superior Academy, where I studied electrical engineering. I made it to the fifteenth level. That was thirty years ago. In those days, the new society was still a little chaotic, so the school administration was a tad stricter with us, allowing us to go home only once every three months. Since my parents had passed away a long time ago, I stayed at school, unable to understand the changes going on outside. Occasionally I'd hear something from one of my classmates. In those days, the mass media consisted of television and newspapers. For some reason I never understood, the authorities shut down the papers and thereby completely controlled the news. You could only see the most 'constructive' reports. But from my classmates, I learned that some massive purge was getting under way outside. Later, the professor told me he'd had a similar experience—the purge made it to the school and a number of classmates and professors disappeared, without it ever being thoroughly investigated. In this way, I quietly finished my course of study at the academy. After graduating, I began working at the Department of Electrical Engineering in the Ministry of Industry. I got to know Professor Kang not so much because I was interested in history, but rather because during vacations when all the other students had gone home, I stayed alone on campus with no place to go, and the old professor was always alone as well."

When Du Qun finished his story, he looked at Xi De as if waiting for him to ask him something.

"Then how did you come to be sent to Industrial City?" Xi De couldn't help asking.

"That's a long story. . . ."

At that moment, Lian Lian came in, interrupting their conversation. She told Xi De that someone was holding a party and that she hoped Du could go with them. Finally the three of them left Xi De's place and went to another building.

Since there were so many people at the party, all they did was drink. By the end of the party, Lian Lian was thoroughly drunk. Xi De took her home before returning to his own place, where he discovered Du waiting at his door.

"Didn't get enough to drink, right?" said Du, patting him on the shoulder. "Why not come to my place? I have some green liquor."

Perhaps Xi De had not had enough to drink, or that bottle of green liquor was pretty tempting; at any rate, they set off for Du's place.

Du lived in an old-style two-story building down a side lane. It was damp and dark. Du explained that everyone else had moved to a new high-rise with the latest electrical facilities on the main street. But he was used to everything in the old building and was able to prevent it from being torn down after quite a bit of running around.

Du showed Xi De every room; there were a number of appliances Xi De had never seen. They paused at one garret where a thick, fleecy lambskin rug was spread on the floor. It was furnished with a bed, two bookcases, and a rocking chair. Du turned on an old table lamp; the yellowish light seemed to send the room back in time several decades.

"Where'd you get all the books?" asked Xi De.

"I found them in a cellar," said Du, sitting down in the rocking chair. "Let's have a drink. This green liquor was smuggled in from Central City."

They clinked glasses in a toast. Xi De took a sip and, holding his glass, walked over to the bookcases.

"These books were all printed thirty or forty years ago, when there was still a publishing industry. With the exception of a few light novels, they're all books of specialized knowledge. They've all been digitized and are nothing special."

"Is this where you kill time?"

"I don't have much interest in computer games. Sometimes I'll go to a party to see people." Du continued, "Didn't you ask me why I was sent to Industrial City?"

"If you don't feel like telling . . ."

"It's all right," he said, lifting his glass. "It's a lot better than it used to be. People can talk freely, but there are fewer and fewer things to talk about. There'll come a day when people in different professions won't be able to talk to each other."

"That's quite possible," said Xi De, in total agreement.

"This is how it happened. After graduating from the academy, I, like all other young people, both indecisively and with some aspirations, went to work for the Ministry of Industry. At that time, the Minister of Industry was Mo Zhao. He was the youngest minister, and the reason I mention him is that he is entirely responsible for having me sent here. At that time, the new society was slowly beginning to regain some calm after the second purge and starting to come to order. A lot of opportunities awaited progressive young people. The first regional committee members had already served 30 or 40 years and they were all utterly senile. Under those circumstances, the demand for new elections was becoming more vocal. Young people like us, who had just graduated, were filled with enthusiasm and eager to do things. For this reason we were 100 percent behind Mo Zhao, who was barely 40 years old then, and we were ready to shed our blood and lay down our lives for him. This went on for three years until the shocking news that Max Kristen, the chairman of the Central Committee, had only recently passed away after having lived to the ripe old age of 100. Not long thereafter, the second chairman, Ge Tingguang, who succeeded Max Kristen, issued an order demanding that new elections be held for the ten regional committees, and any committee member over 80 had to retire. The regional committee elections weren't entirely democratic because the middle and lower classes didn't really understand anything about the administrative class, so the right to vote was given to the various department cadres. With our vigorous support,

Mo Zhao was easily elected to the regional committee and was the youngest committee member."

Xi De was fascinated by all this. Twenty years later, Mo Zhao had become the chairman of the regional committee and a member of the central committee. His picture hung in every meeting room in Central City. But no one knew anything about his past. In the new society, the regional committees had the highest policy-making authority. Although the members had absolute authority, they withdrew behind the scenes. They did not need to have any contact with the people, and through a vast network of computers they controlled every department. Occasionally they would address the people via their television screens. So Chairman Mo Zhao actually did have a past.

"After Mo Zhao was easily elected, those of us who supported him all received some benefit. I became the head of the Department of Electrical Engineering under the Ministry of Industry and was in charge of the electricity of three cities. At that time I was really an arrogant young man. Mo Zhao often saw us in his official residence, but such circumstances couldn't continue for long. He realized that he didn't really have to meet with the various departments in person; all he had to do was issue his commands via computer. Thus, Mo Zhao seemed to vanish from before us. When he wanted to issue an order or hear a report, a computer set up in our homes would beep. Onscreen, Mo Zhao was always dressed the same and maintained the same expression. As far as I can determine, his appearance onscreen hasn't changed in the slightest in over twenty years. Now let me repeat what I said before. I can say that my rise to department head was a matter of high spirits and a bright future. What's more, the following year, I took my first vacation. The Bureau of Character Readjustment under the Ministry of Education had just been established, and I was among the first group of officials to go on vacation. My destination was New City, Australia. Have you heard of it?"

Xi De shook his head. He also noticed how Du's eyes seemed to shine.

"New City is an enchanting place, and I'll never forget it for as long as I live, because that's where I met Liana. Liana, my goddess! Liana, my dream! Her purity, her beauty, her frown, her smile, still appear today in my dreams. During the month we were together, our souls grew closer by the day. The harmony that increased by the day ultimately reached an indescribable stage. My one-month vacation passed quickly. I couldn't bear to return to Central City. After returning, I spent every day trying to realize my fervent hope of regaining Liana. I pleaded with everyone who might have some influence, especially those in the Ministry of Education. In those days the doors were not as tightly shut as they are today. But all to no avail. Finally, I had no choice but to ask Mo Zhao, which I did one day after he contacted me via computer about an electrical matter. The moment he appeared, I cried and pleaded with him to intercede on my behalf. At the time, he seemed genuinely moved. I saw him nod, and then the screen went blank."

Du's expression at recalling sweet memories began to fade and give way to one of revenge and pain.

"Six months later, I saw Liana. She had arranged every detail. We met briefly in the train station of Central City. According to Liana, six months before, Mo Zhao had suddenly flown to New City—regional committee members could go anyplace at any time—and asked for her by name. Later she was taken back to Central City, where she became Mo Zhao's woman. Our meeting lasted all of ten minutes and when we parted, Liana asked me to forget her and to move on. I was heartbroken! After that, I started to drink. There wasn't a day I didn't get stinking drunk until they finally sent me here."

The room suddenly seemed filled with sadness. Xi De looked at the middle-aged man before him with sympathy.

"That's the end of the story," said Du Qun, forcing a laugh.

They sat in silence for a while. Du poured Xi De another glass of green wine.

"What about you?" asked Du.

Being somewhat in his cups, Xi De told him about Zhen.

"This is just one reason you are unable to pull yourself together, isn't it?" asked Du, fixing his gaze on Xi De. "There's got to be another reason."

Xi De was startled by Du's perspicacity. He thought it over before replying: "Why are you so interested in me?"

Du knew what he was referring to.

"I've been interested in you since the first time I saw you," muttered Du, while cautiously examining Xi De's every expression. "I've had my eyes on you, your cold, sober look, the cautious way you keep your distance from others, the constant careful way you have with everything. Finally, I came to the conclusion that we are the same. Both of us harbor enormous secrets."

"What secret?" asked Xi De.

"It's a secret that makes you different from others," said Du, standing up and walking to the window, "but it also makes you feel uneasy, and there's no one you can speak with to get it off your chest. I had the very same feeling when I left Central City. Overnight, my ideals and any meaning were destroyed, but even more painful was that I had fought for a liar for so long."

Du Qun walked over to Xi De and regarded him in all earnestness and sincerity.

"I'm the only person in whom you can put your trust."

It was clear to Xi De now. Du didn't tell just anyone he met about his hatred for Chairman Mo Zhao. He also recalled the old professor's expression when he mention Du Qun's name. The wrinkled, age-spotted face was filled with sadness and deep concern. Perhaps the old professor could foresee the fates of these two students to whom he was closest.

"I once mentioned what was puzzling me to the old professor. He mentioned your name and thought perhaps you—"

"Why didn't you come to see me earlier?"

"I was confused for a while," said Xi De, shaking his head. "After all, I had received sixteen years of Central Academy education. I had just taken my place in society and thought everything was wonderful. I didn't have to exert myself in the least when it came to life, work, play, or thought—everything had been well planned. Wasn't this the Heaven described by generations of thinkers? But on the verge of mindlessly throwing myself into the relentlessly turning wheels of this giant machine, I had second thoughts, something happened. . . ."

"What happened?" asked Du anxiously.

At that point, Xi De began to narrate how he had discovered Winston and his book *The True Face of the Central Committee*. Du listened, enthralled, the expressions on his face shifting, by turns smiling and gloomy, but never once interrupting his narrative.

"Just think of what a shock it gave me," Xi De finally said, "to discover what no one dared to believe: the great Max Kristen was a scoundrel, a cheat, and a mad idealist. And the Supreme Committee was a violent, cruel, and evil organization with blood-soaked hands."

"Notwithstanding the fact that you discovered the book through an unusual dream, it's all quite believable. Xi De, do you believe what Winston said?"

"Naturally I was skeptical at first, believing the book to be part of a plot or the product of a raving madman."

"And later? How did you deal with it?"

"Although reason told me that I couldn't have complete faith, my thoughts did undergo an unconscious shift. I began to come out of my 'inherent life' and to examine the outside world with curiosity and alertness. Then one Sunday, I couldn't resist going to see the old professor."

"What did he say?"

"He believed that Winston had done everything in his power to cross space and time to locate a redeemer and what he found was me, a pure and innocent but confused child." Xi De laughed. "But the professor believed that Winston's accusations were for the most part true, because the detonations of nuclear weapons in various places in those days seemed to be planned. He also mentioned an anti-Nanning organization in those days."

Du appeared to sympathize and understand as he listened to Xi De describe his confusion and uneasiness with regard to the entire system, the impact his vacation and Zhen had had on him, as well as his impressions of the lower-class residents of the industrial city.

"The new society is not all it is cracked up to be superficially, right?" asked Du.

Xi De nodded.

"All right. I'm going to take you someplace where you can learn a lot more, for which you are qualified."

21

It was the basement of the building. Du Qun led Xi De along the exposed water and ventilation pipes, coming to a halt before a large, rusty compressor.

"This is an old-style emergency electrical generator. It's no longer used."

Du felt around on the wall and pushed on a depression, which started a loud rumbling. It was a door.

"This is an old atomic bomb shelter built a long time ago." Du led Xi De down a flight of steps as the door closed behind them.

They found themselves in a small metallic room. Du flipped a switch and immediately the room was filled with a bright light. Xi De saw several old machines and a small screen on the wall.

"Have a seat here," said Du, as he turned on an old projector. "Let's watch a film clip first."

The room grew dark, and one image after another appeared on the screen.

"That's a nuclear device exploding in an Indian state as photographed from the air."

After the explosion, all the buildings had been leveled. The camera panned upward, the background growing dark, and finally came to rest on something that resembled a wheel.

"What's that?"

"That's a space station. See the letters U.S.A. written on it? It was photographed accidentally by a Japanese commercial satellite."

"What is that large disclike object protruding there?"

"That is Nanning." A burst of blinding light suddenly shot from the disc. "It's exploding the nuclear weapons on earth."

Xi De watched, amazed and speechless.

"Let's watch it again."

A group of people armed with automatic weapons appeared onscreen and were firing on a building. At that moment, in the lower left-hand part of the screen appeared a gray armored vehicle, on top of which was mounted a needle- or pipelike object; then there were bursts of bright light.

"Using a 'blitz weapon,' this instance of anti-Nanning violence was wiped out in ten seconds."

Du turned off the projector. In the dark, Xi De listened to his solemn voice, totally lacking in emotion.

"This clip proves everything you already know: the new society was built on a bloody massacre. But history tells us that during any revolution blood will flow, and some people will always have to be sacrificed in the founding of a new system. If the new system is good, then settling old scores does nothing to help the situation save to satisfy the ethical feelings of a few individuals." Agreeing with his point of view, Xi De nodded. "But the issue here is not the bloody means by which these people were eliminated, but . . ."

Du paused at this point to turn on the light. In the bright light, Xi De's young face was flushed red.

"Have you heard of the Defend the Earth Army?"

"Yes, in the Steel District. It seems to be an organization bent on stirring up trouble."

"Not many people really understand what the Defend the Earth Army is all about," said Du, sighing. "I'm the commander of the Defend the Earth Army in the Third Industrial City."

"Huh?"

"It's hard to believe that the organization predates the Supreme Committee. As for it being bent on stirring up trouble, as you say, that is just a few marginal elements of the Defend the Earth Army, a few bored and disgruntled lower-class people we have been able to manipulate. The genuine members of the Defend the Earth Army are scattered throughout the middle and upper classes, where they are well concealed. The membership of the Defend the Earth Army is declining because talent is hard to come by and very few are willing to accept the beliefs we hold," said Du. "I'm sure you have a lot of questions now. What the heck is the Defend the Earth Army? What are we defending? What on earth has to be defended? Are we defending the earth against aliens?"

Du seemed to savor the unparalleled astonishment and confusion written all over Xi De's face. After a while, he took a stack of photographs out of a drawer.

"Have a look at these photos first."

Xi De took the stack of old, yellowing photographs.

"They're all flying machines. Why?"

"Right, but in those days they were called flying saucers."

"When were these taken?"

"Fifty years ago."

"Jeez," said Xi De, raising his voice, "they look just like the ones today."

"These photos were collected by several aerospace scientists, the founders of the Defend the Earth Army."

"You're saying that they thought aliens from outer space wanted to invade the earth?"

"They've already invaded."

"How's that possible?"

"We have reason to believe that Nanning is a scheme of theirs."

"That's inconceivable," said Xi De, standing up. First it was Winston, then the old professor's story, then the encounter with Du Qun, and at last this unbelievable, if not mythical Defend the Earth Army.

"Have a seat, Xi De, and listen closely to what I have to say," said Du, his voice becoming low and filled with emotion. "I am now going to reveal to you one of the greatest mysteries of human civilization. We have lost a lot of people assembling this information, but the sacrifices have been worth it. In spite of everything, they were willing to risk untold danger, even to secure a brief written passage, offering their lives as if they meant nothing. I have photocopies of everything here, which you can look at in a moment."

When Commander Du began to recount his historical view of human civilization, the air in the room seemed suddenly to take on a chill and grow still. The four walls reflected the bright and silent lamplight, and it felt as if thousand of eyes were staring coldly. A shiver ran up his spine as Xi De was overcome by an atmosphere of absolute terror.

"In the past, there were a number of ways to explain human history. One was the religious view of history, which held that the development of humanity was part of God's divine plan for the universe, an as yet unsolved riddle. The second was the political view of history, which held that the decisive forces in the past were the kings, nobles, lawmakers, and soldiers. The third was the heroic view of history, which was closely related to the political view of history, because in general, the heroes of history came from among the great nobles, kings, generals, lawmakers, founders of nations, pioneer reformers, and revolutionaries. The fourth was the ideological view of history, which held that ideology was the main reason for historical progress and that the material conditions of society were arrived at by means of certain galvanizing ideas. The fifth is the economic view of history, which held that human life was supported by goods and labor and that the exchange of goods and labor was the basis of all social development and structure.

"But what I want to say is that all of these ideas are possible explanations derived from limited information. What's the truth, then? What are the origin and future of humanity? I will reveal this ancient mystery now.

"Long, long ago, when the earth was just a dull clod lying idly by, all sorts of strange animals crawled over its surface. It is clear that had it not been for outside interference, the animals would have maintained their original forms to this very day. Take, for example, the apes and lions in the forests of Africa. Despite the vastness of time or even the brilliant theory of the evolution of species, the apes would still be apes and the lions, lions thousands of years hence as they were thousands of years ago. The ants of today are identical to those of hundreds of thousands of years ago. If there was no outside interference, then why is it that one species of ape—man—evolved at an astonishing pace when all other species seem to have been fixed and not evolving? Well, what do I mean by outside interference?

"At one end of the universe is a planet on which lived a form of intelligent life. One day, tens of thousands of years ago, the planet dispatched a fleet of spaceships to cross the Milky Way on a mission. One spaceship, owing to mechanical difficulties or some other unknown reason, found itself lost on earth. When the aliens disembarked, they discovered that they had landed on a beautiful, though hopelessly primordial planet. Their ship was beyond repair, and the fleet had abandoned all hope of locating any survivors and was on its way home. Under these circumstances, the lost aliens had to think of something in this ridiculous place. Fortunately, the primordial planet produced countless species of animals and concealed rich mineral deposits. But the lucky survivors and their advanced instruments were not able to come up with a means of returning home to their highly industrialized civilization. What were they to do?

"After many discussions, a large, long-term and time-consuming, nearly perfect plan was decided upon. The first step in this plan was to start from the very beginning. They selected several species of apes and operated on these simple beasts surgically. Thus a controlled mutation occurred: a simple *Homo sapiens* prototype was implanted in the mind of a remote human ancestor. After that, the birth of the true human, able to reason, assess, engage in animal husbandry, and make tools followed. With environmental adaptations, man began to migrate and establish villages, and finally inhabited all parts of the world. In response to special regional conditions, unique cultures appeared. As populations increased, culture continued to develop until it reached a certain stage. Competitive behavior resulted from increasingly frequent contacts among populations and the overlapping of living environments. The early competition acted as a constructive stimulus. Perhaps the aliens intended to produce this stimulus in a surreptitious fashion by, for example, implanting certain suitable ideas in the subconscious of a few exceptional individuals.

"When the stimulus reached the point of explosion, war occurred. Although war brought disaster, reduction in population, and material destruction, it also indirectly achieved the goal of allowing the new to supersede the old. In order to reduce the destructiveness of war, the aliens then created the various faiths as well as idealism in the guise of religion. Naturally, this was through a number of famous wise people. These chosen earthlings came up with towering theories overnight. We can point to a number of ideas that changed the course of history as proof. The process of producing these ideas is mysterious and difficult to explain. The founders of many religions, for example, claim that their original ideas came to them in their dreams or through divine inspiration. Many important scientists have also explained that their discoveries happened unexpectedly, through a stroke of genius or a brainstorm. Therefore, on the heels of a major war, a leap in human civilization can take place. Time advances, and sometimes, in order to solve a problem or simply to check the record, the aliens have appeared at a certain point in a certain age. Contemporary witnesses often record in their histories, 'the god visited' or 'celestial phenomena occurred,' or 'Apollo stood on the western horizon,' 'amid thunder, God led Moses across the Red Sea' and the like. In recent times, with increased population and mobility, each unique culture reached maturity, the Greek, Egyptian, and Islamic, for example. Through the blending of these formed cultures and through cultural cross-fertilization, a living, moving modern civilization was produced.

"The aliens occupied a controlling position, but out of view behind the screen. They created regional conflicts and brought about the unification of many important factors such as blood lineage, language, religion, and custom. Then, selecting representative peoples or those with potential to develop, they helped them to achieve certain things culturally, such as the improvement in production preceding the industrial revolution, or relying on Bacon to help bring about the scientific revolution. The outbreak of the First World War helped to increase the speed of industrialization of several advanced countries. This was followed shortly by the Second World War, and the resultant losses and damage from the conflict, which dwarfed the first, were astonishing, but also allowed the second wave of industrialization to reach its peak. In the thirty or forty years after the war, scientific and technical developments surpassed all those from the previous history of humankind. But then a huge problem reared its head: when industrialization reaches a certain level, world wars will always end in common ruin. At the same time, population pressures, environmental degradation, and the breakdown of reason all served to propel us toward global Armageddon.

"At that time, in order to reduce the stimulus on man, the aliens stopped appearing and designed Nanning. We have reason to believe that Max Kristen was not an earthling. After Nanning began to play its given role, the earth at a given time lost 90 percent of its undesirable population and 80 percent of its second-class construction. Then came the final stage of industrialization, which was unlike the previous three stages in that it was better planned and more precisely controlled. Its goal was the establishment of a pure and highly mechanized civilization, in which machines would gradually replace human beings. According to reliable data, the world's population is declining annually. We have learned of some factory workers being eliminated. They suddenly and mysteriously vanished. Many technicians replaced by machines also disappeared, their whereabouts unknown. These are frightening circumstances. We believe that if people do not do something quickly, a day will come, and in the not too distant future, when the whole human race will disappear from the face of the earth. The only thing left will be a high-tech factory controlled by aliens or machines that will be capable of producing the means of crossing the Milky Way. We believe that the aliens do not possess the ethics, character, or goodwill that they gave the people of the earth. As far as they are concerned, humanity is just an incubator to produce machines; we are nothing more than white rats in a lab. This is an age-old hoax—the meaning of human existence is nothing but a bad joke, and God's will is . . . just a pat on the backside when everything is accomplished."

Du paused, his eyes fixed on the stunned Xi De. He slowly drained his glass and continued:

"We are in no way resigned to this fate. Although we are tools, we are in no way resigned to being used and then discarded—this is the existential imperative of the Defend the Earth Army."

The room grew silent as the sound of Du's voice faded. They looked at each other, their eyes filled with sadness and hopelessness. After a while, Xi De could be heard flipping through the old documents. They were the investigative reports of the Defend the Earth Army research conducted over many years. Xi De's expression changed repeatedly under the light of the lamp.

Finally, the sound of turning pages ceased.

"I'm willing to join you," said Xi De, pronouncing each word distinctly.

The following day, Xi De met the core members of the Defend the Earth Army in the same place. They came from different work units. One of them, who appeared to be from the opposite shore, had sneaked into the Administrative District.

In the presence of these comrades, Xi De took a simple yet solemn oath to the army. After this, Commander Du affixed a false and transparent fingernail to his hand.

"If captured, swallow this fingernail and you will be able to destroy all of your brain cells in a matter of a couple of seconds. This is the glorious martyrdom only the comrades of the core group are honored to possess," said the commander. "Ordinary members of the army are normally not qualified to know our secrets. Most of them are young and can be roused as a group when needed."

"Commander, what is my duty at present?"

"Your duty at present is to make a move when the time is right or to keep an eye out for disgruntled colleagues. It's not your responsibility to recruit them, because convincing others to join the Defend the Earth Army is difficult. All you need to do is report to us and we'll do the rest. We also feel that your posting to the industrial city is temporary and that there is a good chance you'll be recalled to Central City. This is very important, because the security measures in Central City are much tighter than here. We have lost a lot of comrades there."

"Why is Central City more heavily defended?"

"The Third Industrial City is perhaps on their list to be eliminated," said the commander. "The Steel District, for example, can be eliminated as steel is no longer needed—when all steel buildings have been built or when a new alloy is created that can render the labor-intensive steel industry obsolete."

"I have one question that I'd like to ask the commander," said Xi De. "Is the regional committee already controlled by aliens?"

"That's quite possible. Although we have not been able to infiltrate the highest levels, our observations suggest that not one member has made a public appearance in the last ten years and the images on television are in all likelihood always the same ones."

"What about Chairman Mo Zhao?"

"I would hazard a guess that he was probably the first to be secretly replaced, because after the incident at the Central Train Station, I never again saw Liana or heard anything about her."

22

One year later, Xi De of the Defend the Earth Army was recalled to Central City. When the head of the Bureau of Resource Analysis met his old subordinate, he took a close look at the face of the young man before him. It was uncommonly firm and mature, with two intelligent eyes. The chief sighed and said:

"Welcome back to the bureau. We're giving you Ge Shu's job."

"What about Ge Shu?"

"We found out that he couldn't handle it."

Xi De returned to his dorm. He moved around in the room that had been Ge Shu's. He thought of all that had happened that year and had a vague feeling that some mysterious force had compelled him to experience all these unusual things. He was now a member of the Defend the Earth Army, charged with the important mission of saving the entire human race. The chances of success were near zero, and the way ahead was paved with innumerable hidden dangers. From Du he had acquired an overall understanding of the structure of the new world, something only graduates of the Superior Academy who had received political training knew. But the more he understood, the weightier grew the state of affairs. The upper level of the new world was so tightly closed as to be impenetrable. The Supreme Committee that wielded ultimate power was headquartered in New York. Of the twenty committee members, half were standing members and half were holding concurrent posts as chairmen of the ten regional committees. Regional committees had a total of sixteen members, eight of whom were standing, eight of whom were holding concurrent posts as heads of the ministries of domestic affairs, resources, security, education, industry, agriculture, coordination, and scientific and technological development. The mid-level structure of each ministry was strictly hierarchical; the officials of each level, without exception, contacted their superiors through a computer network, and all administrative orders from the top were, without exception, distributed via computer. For example, the officials of the Ministry of Resources could ascertain via computer the actual situation of a meeting in any subordinate office or in any committee in, say, Resource Analysis. But the officials in Resource Analysis, for their part, did not have access to anything from higher up. They were under orders not to contact their superiors and other offices at the same level, because the use of information technology had replaced any sort of face-to-face contact. Therefore, it was impossible for any sort of class struggle to occur. If revolutionaries were to charge into an office, they would be confronted with an array of complicated and mysterious devices, none of which they would be able to operate. If they wanted to issue an order to occupy, they wouldn't know where to start. If they wanted to locate a high-level official, they wouldn't know who it was or where he lived. Even blowing up the entire section would be of no use because the high-level official would be safe at home and participating in an urgent televised conference from his living room, and via a wireless network would dispatch troops to suppress the revolutionaries. Therefore, in the new world, the definition of revolution was: the capturing of all organizations at the same time by similar numbers of professionals of roughly similar technical ability.

The next day, Xi De made a special trip to the academy to see the old professor, but the people there told him that Kang Zaoshi had died six months earlier. His belongings had all been sent to the incinerator and his ashes had been laid in the Building of Eternal Rest. Xi De made his way to the fifty-floor building, took the elevator to the twenty-third floor, and located the professor's name on a drawer mounted in the wall. He stood in silence for several minutes. He felt he was standing in front of a huge bookcase. Death momentarily became an immense joke, a senseless nightmare. Then he left the building without so much as a backward glance.

That Sunday afternoon found Xi De standing beneath the bronze statue of Max Kristen in the city park, where he met the Defend the Earth Army contact person. After cautiously confirming their identities, they walked along the path skirting the lake. At that time a number of youngsters were sailing their remote-controlled boats. The colorful electronic contraptions cut through the water in pursuit of one another.

"I have orders from above. Tonight you are expected to attend a meeting in the number twelve game room in the bar on the third floor of the Agricultural Building. This is your ID card."

It was a false ID for an employee of the Ministry of Agriculture. Xi De shoved it into his pocket.

"I am responsible solely for this preliminary contact. At the meeting someone else will inform you as to your mission in Central City," he said, stretching out his hand. "So long and good luck."

The bar was filled with employees of the Ministry of Agriculture. Passing through groups of laughing men and women, Xi De made his way to the number twelve game room. A man standing at the door stretched out his arm and prevented him from entering.

"I'm sorry, but the Ahka Game is already full."

Xi De gave the password and was permitted to enter. The door closed behind him. Six people sat in the room. On the video screen mounted in the wall were the words "Ahka Game." It was a game in which two teams played at star wars. The players were sitting and punching their keyboards while on the screen appeared all sorts of strange weapons, in hot pursuit of one another. The whole thing was accompanied by exciting music. People often played till they were covered with sweat and totally oblivious to all else. Xi De nodded to each comrade by way of greeting. Thus the meeting began amid the raucous sounds of the Ahka game.

First, a middle-aged man sitting to the right in front stood up and said:

"Comrades, let me introduce you the new blood of the Fifth Action Group, Xi De, the Resource Analyst."

Xi De raised himself in a show of respect.

Following this, the leader introduced the six other members. In addition to the group leader, who was a mid-level official in the Welfare Section of the Ministry of Domestic Affairs, there was his assistant, a low-level clerk of the Ministry of Industry; a street cleaner; two waste-disposal technicians; the manager of a bar attached to the Ministry of Education; and a city bus driver.

Xi De examined his partners in revolution and couldn't help feeling a little disappointed because they were not really paying attention to the group leader's lengthy introductory remarks. They were hitting the buttons on their keyboards, causing wildly funny images to appear on the screen accompanied by explosions and flashes, which made the street cleaner open his mouth in a hideous smile. The bus driver narrowed his eyes as he sized up Xi De, as if suspicious about why he had showed up at the meeting.

"The Fifth Action Group has been around for five years. In that time, we have gathered a lot of good intelligence, including a blueprint of the Central City Recreation Zone and the location of the Ministry of Scientific and Technological Development. Of course we have lost several comrades, but for the future of mankind, their sacrifice was unavoidable. We are happy to have Comrade Xi De join us today. He spent one year with Mr. Du, that great revolutionary theorist of the Defend the Earth Army...."

That was the first time Xi De had heard Du referred to as a great revolutionary theorist. He felt strange.

After the group leader finished his talk, the clerk took over, saying:

"I report to the group leader. We have repeatedly requested precision weapons from above. Why has nothing happened?"

"Headquarters has always believed that armed violence is the final solution," explained the leader in an amiable manner.

An expletive was heard near Xi De.

"What do you have to say, Zong Xuan?" Zong Xuan was none other than the street cleaner.

"I admit that theory is important, but what good is theory if there is no real action?"

"Let's hear the new comrade's opinion."

Xi De considered the question before responding:

"I believe that our army cannot act recklessly at this time, because given our strength we would be able to occupy just a few insignificant organizations."

Initially he had wanted to tell them that armed action was impossible.

"But through action, we can awaken the people," said one of the waste disposal technicians indignantly, pounding on his game board. The screen emitted a number of static bleeps. "I've waited eleven years for this day, in this foul garbage heap. My life is not as comfortable as that of an academy graduate like you, who can spend all day talking. I don't want to spend my whole life waiting here...."

The group leader motioned to him to stop complaining.

"I'll take this matter to the higher-ups."

After the meeting ended, the group leader invited Xi De to have a drink. They took a corner of the bar.

"If I don't give them a chance to blow off steam once in a while," said the group leader, sighing, "something will happen sooner or later."

"But Commander Du told me—"

"You still don't get it, Xi De. Not one of them buys this whole story about being invaded by aliens from outer space."

"Goodness!"

"With the exception of a few core comrades of the Defend the Earth Army, most members have joined because they are dissatisfied with their jobs or some other personal reason."

"Then how can the revolution—"

"We have to be resigned to our fate," said the group leader. "They're even dissatisfied with you and me."

"What are we going to do?"

"We must gain access to a high-level agency."

"But that's too difficult."

"Sending you to an action group was a mistake on the part of head-quarters," said the group leader apologetically. "We are incapable of doing anything except complaining."

23

The action group was not the place for someone as ardent and purposeful as Xi De. Their meetings were nothing more than gripe sessions, and there was no future for their efforts. After joining the Defend the Earth Army, they became acquainted with the lifestyle of the upper class and came to envy and hate them, and put down the ideals of the great army. However, according to Du's theory, at the beginning of overthrowing the leadership class, only the unthinking masses were capable of bringing into full play the unbridled power of the revolution, and only could those who were passionate about the revolution actually placate the uneasy people. Du believed that a lofty goal was of use only for the upper level of revolutionary leadership. History had proven that the masses did not understand any plan to establish a new order. All they could remember were a few slogans such as, "Down with the landlords" and "Down with official corruption." But after the old order was overthrown, then what? Either they were ignorant or they were uninterested. Therefore, after the revolution succeeded, these people would without a doubt become obstacles to the progress of the new society.

What was the likelihood of actually being able to topple the Supreme Committee? Du's reply was disheartening: none. The Ministry of Security of the new world was the most advanced and efficient organization of its kind. Famous security organizations in history included the Russian KGB, Hitler's Gestapo, and the U.S. CIA. They all adopted a method of spy versus spy and always made what ought to have been an easy-to-solve problem into a complicated mess on account of their pathological secrecy. But the Ministry of Security of the new world was different. The overwhelming majority were scholars or experts educated in special skills; they were not the spies in dark glasses and upturned collars of the movies. They wouldn't follow you in the streets or bug your home. Every one of them was gentle and cultivated, polite, modest, and well mannered. Never in a million years would they rush off to put down a rebellion or run around catching revolutionaries. This is because they used "planned insurrection" or "armed rebellion," which is to say they would not just sit back and watch rebellion ferment and break out naturally. They possessed superior information systems and painstaking computer analysis. When the analysis showed that a certain area was likely to erupt in violence at a certain time, they would rush ahead and set off the violence or create a reason for it to erupt. In this way all rebellion was predictable and controllable.

This was frightening. Xi De thought of Du's words while examining his own situation and found it all very troubling. Up to this time, he and his comrades had not encountered the slightest obstacle or the slightest trouble. The Ministry of Security was like an irrelevant shadow on the wall, but he knew that they were somewhere, waiting calmly with a well thought-out plan.

Three months later, Xi De received new orders directing him to leave the action group. The same contact person told him to report to headquarters.

Headquarters was in a basement. There Xi De met the Central City commander, who was an older man around fifty, very thin, with fierce eyes. After scrutinizing Xi De for a moment, he said:

"I saw Commander Du a few days ago and discovered that we had assigned you to the wrong group. The action group is a useless peripheral group. Did you tell them your true identity?"

"I mentioned it," replied Xi De.

"That's too bad," said the commander, "but there is a way to repair the damage. Be a little more careful in the future."

Two other people sat in the background, reading through some documents.

"As you can see," said the commander, directing his eyes to the two men, "core comrades are few in number."

"That's what Commander Du said."

"Therefore we cannot afford to lose even one. Do you know Lin Xing?"

"Lin Xing? We were colleagues at one time."

"He is a core comrade in the agricultural city."

Xi De gasped. He should have known that a discontented middle-aged central official sent down to the countryside would be an ideal recruit for the Defend the Earth Army.

"If nothing untoward happens," said the commander in conclusion, "once a week at an appointed time, go to the bar at the Bureau of Resource Analysis and meet Ah Tai, the bartender. If you have any problems, tell him and he can relay them to us. Do you know Ah Tai?"

Xi De nodded. Of course he knew him, the man who always wore a forced smile and stood behind the bar, ever ready and willing to listen to the drunken maunderings of a customer.

"When something unusual occurs, headquarters will send someone to you."

24

Two months later, Ah Tai came and knocked on his door. Xi De was still half asleep and was startled to see that face with the forced smile. He felt as if he were in the bar.

"You are to go to the riverside tomorrow at noon. Someone wants to meet you," said Ah Tai, standing at the door.

"But—"

"The person knows you."

The following day, Xi De left the Bureau of Resource Analysis alone after lunch and set off toward the river. It was noon, and the buildings on both sides of the street were reflecting a blinding light. Occasional cars would pass silently on the street, but there were few pedestrians.

Xi De sat on a bench beside the river and gazed at the clear blue water flowing beyond his feet. Various matters filled his mind. He envied his colleagues, who had no worries. After work, they would go have fun without any second thoughts, at least not his sort. *Ignorance is bliss*, he suddenly thought. He racked his brain trying to remember where he had heard the expression. At that moment someone slapped him on the shoulders.

"Xi De." It was the commander. "How are you?"

The commander then informed him of an urgent matter that had just occurred. His intelligence indicated that in a few days the Central City Ministry of Coordination would issue an order closing down the Steel-Cutting Plant in the Third Industrial City.

"Three hundred technicians will lose their lives," said the commander, heavily. "You've been to the industrial city and know what it's like. This is an urgent and important mission. Are you willing to go?"

"Yes," replied Xi De, "but how am I supposed to get away from the Bureau of Resource Analysis?"

"Do you remember that computer you fixed last time?" asked the commander, the corner of his mouth twitching. "This time it is in even worse shape, so you'll have to go."

The next day, Xi De did, in fact, receive orders to travel for work. With him, he carried a list of the names of the three hundred low-level technicians that the Ministry of Coordination thought were redundant. Each had mastered only one skill: cutting steel sheets. From morning to night, they squatted and cut out steel plates with a laser gun. If no changes occurred, they, like all other professionals, could live out their lives in a smooth, quiet fashion. But things had changed. Most of the construction for the new world had been completed and there had been a significant drop in demand for steel plates, or perhaps a shearing machine had been invented to take their place. The three hundred workers were like three hundred rusty nails destined to be consigned to the blast furnace. There was no other fate for them. To save them had become the sacred mission of the Defend the Earth Army. But how was it supposed to be accomplished? By opening a new factory to accommodate them?

Xi De sat in the high-speed train bound for the Third Industrial City. The scenery on both sides flew by. His mind moved as swiftly as the scenery.

If he hadn't learned about the secret plan of the aliens to exterminate the people of the earth, then he would probably be sitting calmly behind his desk at work, feeling it was not worth his while to get involved in changes in the outside world. His intellectual training did not include a conscience. But what was a conscience? Ask any academy graduate and he would tell you that acting according to your conscience was just 1 + 1 = 2, a wise activity carried out in the most scientific and efficient fashion. If you asked a bee to live by the dictates of its own conscience, it would laugh at you, because it was not in its character as a bee to complain. In the days when nationalism reigned, the slogan "Sacrifice yourself for the greater good" was viewed as holy writ. But in those days it was just talk; these days, it had been thoroughly inculcated in the new world.

That night, Xi De saw Commander Du and the core comrades in the Administrative District of the industrial city. The situation had become urgent. Du's expression was dignified as he paced the small room.

It was easy to talk about evacuating three hundred people, but it would take nothing less than a miracle to accomplish, and miracles only happened in religious texts.

"What is their current situation?" the commander asked one of his comrades.

"They haven't had anything to do in a week, and some are becoming restless."

"Has anyone been sent to spread rumors?"

"Yes, we dispatched a peripheral comrade to tell them that everyone would be deported to the North Pole."

Perplexed, Xi De shot a glance at Du, who explained softly, "No one believes that they will be 'disappeared.'"

"They would rather die than go to the North Pole."

"What's the response in the Administrative District?"

"None. However, security forces have been sent to the industrial city from other areas and the factory district is under close watch twenty-four hours a day."

"That's troublesome," said Du, shaking his head. "These idiots don't understand a thing. They just want to cause a ruckus."

The meeting continued, and it was finally concluded that the Defend the Earth Army could rescue only thirty people at most. The workers most strongly opposed to the trend of society would be chosen. Given the urgency of the situation, the rescue operation was set for the following night at midnight.

"Xi De, your mission is complete," said Du. "On account of the danger involved, you needn't participate in the rescue operation."

"No, since joining the Defend the Earth Army, I haven't done anything. This time I want to be involved."

Du thought for a moment and said, "Okay. But we hope you will also keep the larger picture in mind. After all, working in Central City is far more important than rescuing a few workers."

"I will," said Xi De, "but where are we going to take them?"

"To the mountains," replied Commander Du. "Our armed forces are all there."

25

After nightfall, the five of them—Commander Du, three core comrades, and Xi De—boarded a small boat and quietly crossed to the other side of the lake. They took a small path and hid from several security patrols along the way until they arrived at the brightly lit streets of the Steel District.

Amid the throngs of people, no one paid them the slightest notice. Finally, they entered an inconspicuous building, where four comrades were already waiting. After shaking hands, the oldest comrade addressed Du:

"Commander, I still favor violence, just to give them a drubbing in any case."

"We can't do that. Do you know how many security forces there are? Anyway, headquarters has decided."

"If that's the way it is, I won't say another word," he said, shrugging his shoulders. "Commander, we're ready."

"Okay," said Du, "this is our rescue route. A truck is waiting for us—it's a truck from the agricultural city used for transporting pigs. It can take us part of the way."

"Is everyone going?" the old comrade asked.

"Xi De and I will go. The rest of you have to cover us."

After quickly discussing the matter, the three who had come with Du and the two others in the room saluted and left one after another.

Four people of relatively higher rank now remained in the room. Du looked around and said:

"I have to make it clear that our mission this time is dangerous. By tomorrow morning, this place will be crawling with security forces. We have to do everything according to schedule, there's not a moment to lose. We're set for eleven tonight—we'll go on foot to where we are supposed to meet the transport truck. At one we will reach the rendezvous point, from where the guerrilla force will take them into the mountains. We must stay alert along the way. The thirty workers are all fools and will be as skittish as rabbits."

"Commander, can we leave now?"

They left together, taking a long way around before finally entering another building. Inside were the thirty workers ready to be evacuated. They each carried a backpack, and their faces were filled with sadness.

"We vow to serve the Defend the Earth Army unto death," mouthed a young comrade, taking the lead.

"We vow to serve the Defend the Earth Army unto death," repeated all the workers together.

After saluting, Du stood in front. In a low, forceful voice, he firmly said:

"Comrades: it is my honor to stand before you today. To be able to work together with you on this worthy project at this historical moment is the proudest moment of my life. This great revolutionary act will certainly be recorded in history. Our descendants will call you the thirty revolutionary comrades from the industrial city . . ."

Xi De listened to Du's openly encouraging and deceitful remarks. Strictly speaking, it was just a bunch of corny expressions such as "mission," "sacred," "great," "ideals," and "glory" heaped together. It was more or less the same as the preaching on television, only it took place in a different location.

Xi De looked over at the faces of the "thirty revolutionary comrades" and saw that their sadness and confusion were gradually being replaced by a flush of excitement and anger. Xi De felt it odd that they could be so quickly and easily affected by such plain and simple words.

The cadence of the commander's voice carried throughout the room. He frequently waved his fist. Every sound and gesture was just right. It seemed quite possible that he had fallen for his own fairy tales.

The speech was followed by a momentary silence, which was in turn followed by thunderous cheers. Du frowned and motioned to them to be quiet.

"Keep quiet, keep quiet," shouted Commander Du, achieving the expected result. "Comrades, check your bags."

"Commander, do we need money?" asked one of them.

"Money is not used in the mountains."

"Commander, can we take wine?"

"Yes, if you can fit it in your bag."

Du patiently answered their many questions. Some were sensible, others were simply childish. When there were no further questions, Du looked at his watch and said, "We should hear a signal any time now."

A minute later they heard a loud siren in the distance. It was a fire alarm. Their "cover" was setting a fire. A lot of running feet were heard outside the door.

The Defend the Earth Army left in an orderly fashion by the back way. In the backyard, the commander moved aside a large flagstone that concealed an underground passage.

"This underground passage has been around for ages," the commander said, turning to Xi De. "It leads outside."

They proceeded by the light of a flashlight. No one uttered a word. After half an hour, they climbed out of the underground passage and found themselves in a forest.

They continued walking. After climbing a hill, they looked back on the factory district at their feet. The whole place was lit by the fire.

"It would only take ten minutes to put out the fire during the day," said Du, "but we found some phosphorus."

On the far side of the hill, a gray highway stretched before them.

"We'll follow this road," said the commander, turning around. "Hurry up. In another hour we'll arrive at the rendezvous point, where the truck will be waiting."

The road was very flat. There was nothing to interrupt them save a few false alarms. In an hour, they saw a container truck parked beside the road in the distance. The commander signaled with his flashlight. Then they proceeded to board the truck in an orderly fashion. The door closed, throwing everyone into utter darkness.

"No one is to speak," said the commander, his voice coming from beside Xi De. "We have to go through two checkpoints, and voices might tip them off."

"Commander," said Xi De, unable to restrain himself, "after we meet with the people in the mountains, will we be returning right away?"

"We'll be coming right back," said Du. "We carried out a similar mission a few years ago, but not as large as this one."

The truck proceeded in silence. Someone seemed to have fallen asleep in the dark and was snoring. Xi De closed his eyes and leaned against the pack of the person beside him. His head was filled with a chaos of images of the meeting, the fire, the speech, and the flight. After a while, he too fell asleep.

26

A strange metallic sound that Xi De seemed to have heard before woke him. He struggled for a moment and opened his eyes. A bright light shone from four sides, hurting his eyes. He raised his hand to block the light.

"Where am I? What is this place?" he muttered.

The light slowly dimmed and Xi De lowered his hand. He could see clearly now. He was sitting on a sofa in the middle of an otherwise empty room. It was a shiny metal room, brightly lit. The light came from a shining sheet of metal in the ceiling. There was no door or windows. He didn't know what time it was, whether it was day or night. He didn't know what had happened. Perhaps it was just a dream. He shook his head and closed his eyes for a moment. When he opened his eyes, everything was the same. It was no dream. Everything around him, the cold, metallic walls and the abnormal atmosphere of the room, was all real.

Confusion, unease, and fear swept over him. Xi De tried to get up from the sofa, but found his limbs unresponsive and had to give up the idea of standing. Paralyzed, he waited for something to happen.

In perhaps another hour or so, that metallic sound again recalled him from his trancelike condition.

"Xi De, wake up." The voice emanated from the wall facing him.

Xi De shuddered, opened his eyes, and fixed them on a strange image that was materializing on the wall. The overhead light slowly dimmed. Suddenly the wall became a huge screen. On the screen a person sat at a desk with his back turned. He was dressed in a gray uniform Xi De had never seen before. Under his startled gaze, the chair suddenly turned toward him. As the camera slowly zoomed in, the person's face grew larger until it filled the screen. It was a terrifying image and made Xi De's hair stand on end. The face had been so enlarged that every pore, wrinkle, and even the saliva at the corners of his mouth were clearly visible. As the face was fixed on the screen, the gray background gradually turned black and in contrast, the man's face took on a deathly gray patina. His facial features looked artificial and inflexible. He looked like a face on a wrinkled banknote. Only his eyes displayed any anger. Xi De looked away in order to avoid those piercing eyes.

"Xi De, do you know where you are?"

A reply crossed his mind at once, but he shook his head.

"You are at the Ministry of Security." The face remained expressionless.

Although Xi De had suspected as much, he was still startled.

"How come? How could I—"

"In this new world where civilization has reached its technological pinnacle," the metallic voice continued, "the most advanced, newest, and most effective security ministry in history is actually overlooked by most people. It's inconceivable. Xi De, although you had heard of our existence, you still had your doubts. You only saw a few kind and genial security police, who would never do anything more than check your ID. Even your intelligence activities in the park seemed not to attract the slightest notice; nor did your public dissatisfaction or complaints about the authorities draw attention. This resulted in a misperception on your part. You believed that even if the Ministry of Security existed, it was nothing more than a third-rate organization that did nothing."

Xi De was silent.

"But of the eight ministries under the Supreme Committee, the Ministry of Security is the largest, tightest, and most effective. For most people, a government's security measures consist of nothing but a few spies, undercover agents, eavesdropping, interrogations, and other activities. But the definition of 'security' in the new world is completely different. You don't have to worry about being beaten, given electric shocks, or tortured in other ways. We are not interested in such out-of-date methods, because we are omniscient and omnipresent."

At this point, the face suddenly smiled.

"You must be filled with doubt and have a lot of questions you'd like to ask, right?"

Xi De nodded. One smile and the atmosphere of the entire room relaxed a bit.

"What happened to the others?" he asked.

"The container truck you boarded was sent by our Ministry of Security. It didn't take you to the rendezvous point, but to Central City."

"This is Central City?"

"Where did you think it was?" replied the face. "I may as well tell you that you are in the Administrative Building."

The Administrative Building! It was the very symbol of Central City, and he could see it from his own office window. The building housed not only the all-powerful regional committees but also the Ministry of Security.

As the situation became clearer, Xi De's mind revived; the fear and confusion of a moment ago had vanished. He had to bestir himself. He had no illusions about his situation: he was a prisoner. The same could probably be said for his comrades, but why hadn't they been locked up together? Perhaps the Ministry of Security planned to extract something from them. If, as the face said, the Ministry of Security knew everything, then there was no point in speaking with him. They would in all likelihood throw him in prison or some other place. Something was up. Perhaps they wanted the location of the Defend the Earth Army headquarters. Perhaps it was still safe. That was the last hope. He had to deal cautiously with the difficult situation facing him.

"Who are you?"

"I thought you'd never ask," said the face, smiling. "I am the assistant director of the Ministry of Security."

"And what about my companions?"

"They are no longer needed by the new world; therefore they are easier to deal with." He talked as if he were referring to something insignificant.

"Is the elimination of the steel-cutting plant true then?"

"Yes, Xi De. Do you sympathize with them?"

"They are people too."

"Oh, you have been brainwashed by the Defend the Earth Army."

"I wasn't brainwashed," said Xi De, leaning forward. In all sincerity he addressed the face. "Please listen to me. This is an ancient plot."

"What?"

"Listen closely to what I have to say, Assistant Director. Aliens from outer space have already invaded the earth, and the Supreme Committee is under their control. They are planning at this moment to eliminate all earthlings."

But unexpectedly, the assistant director was not startled.

"Xi De, this is the grand goal of your Defend the Earth Army, right?"

"Assistant Director, you have to believe me. Please believe me before it is too late."

The large eyes on the screen met Xi De's.

"At first we were going to let you leave with your grand and lofty ideals, because we have a certain responsibility for you." The pair of eyes seemed to take on a look of compassion. "You are a talented, high-level professional of the new society, superior to workers and farmers . . ."

"Assistant Director, you must believe me."

"No, Xi De, you have been poisoned. Although we have to take some responsibility, we have always provided you with opportunities. We allowed you to have contact with the lower class, we let you see that the Defend the Earth Army is nothing but rabble and that Du's theories are nothing more than the ravings of a lunatic. But you, you have persisted out of sheer stubbornness in intentionally ignoring how the new society operates as a whole while clinging to the parts you prefer, paying attention to a few insignificant problems. You listen to the occasional complaints in a bar and then you actually fail to observe that most people live lives of peace and serenity, and are largely free from want. You have seen the young people having fun in the park and you have seen the happy spectators at the regatta; their happiness and excitement are in no way false. You've seen all of this, but you never thought about it. Instead you intentionally exaggerate the normal job fatigue of a couple of people, you prefer to feel sorry for a few workers who lost their jobs, and you look askance at the continuous and ongoing accomplishments of civilization. So you fall under the spell of the ludicrous and laughable revolutionary theories of the Defend the Earth Army. Xi De, we are disappointed in you."

He doesn't believe me, sadly thought Xi De. *He doesn't believe that humanity is on the road to extinction.*

"As I just said, there was originally no need to have this conversation with you. But you rebelled against the new society. With our full knowledge, we don't need to interrogate you; all we need to do is turn you over to the Bureau of Law Enforcement. But as we are responsible for you, we believe that we should give you one more chance to correct your thinking and return again to the bosom of the new society."

"You're planning to extract the location of Defend the Earth Army headquarters from me, right?"

Xi De glanced furtively at his little finger. Perhaps suicide was the only way out.

"We've already removed the nail from your little finger."

Goodness! It was all over now. Xi De lifted his head, his eyes sad and hopeless.

"We've known the whereabouts of the Defend the Earth Army headquarters for ages. I'll tell you the address."

The address was correct. Xi De made no reply. He was overcome with despair.

I should have known, thought Xi De. *They hypnotized me while I was in a stupor. This conversation is nothing but a game of cat and mouse, which they are perhaps filming for an instructional movie titled* The Awakening of a Rebel.

"Let me tell you: we are familiar with every move of the Defend the Earth Army in the mountains and the city."

He's lying, he's reading his lines, thought Xi De.

"You must wonder why we allow the Defend the Earth Army to exist and continue causing problems. The answer is simple. The Defend the Earth Army is a constant lure that must exist as long as humanity has not progressed to a stage of perfection, but it must exist according to our plans. We know that human beings are of two contradictory minds: on the one hand, they are obedient; on the other hand, they are rebellious. But more often than not, in a tightly structured organization, the former tends to force the latter into the background. But rebelliousness has not necessarily disappeared. In a small number of cases, this structure will make them more cautious and tricky. The tighter the organization, the more frightening the rebelliousness can become. We have always realized the seriousness of this situation; therefore, we never allow rebellion to ferment and mature. We take the initiative in a timely fashion and bring it out. This is why the Defend the Earth Army must exist. Simultaneously, we provide the Defend the Earth Army with ridiculous revolutionary ideals, such as 'Aliens have invaded the earth, the Defend the Earth Army will rescue the earth.' Since the masses are by and large ignorant, we cannot take risks lightly. We cannot allow the Defend the Earth Army to have lofty ideals with which to attract the masses. With such ridiculous slogans, they will find it difficult to mobilize people. If they are not wholehearted believers, they are absolute unbelievers. The masses are fence-sitters, they will not go along simply on an impulse.

This is why the Defend the Earth Army has been able to exist all along, to help us make the new supersede the old."

He's lying again, thought Xi De.

The assistant director paused for a moment and looked at Xi De, as if searching his expression.

"I'm sure you think that I am lying or trying to deceive you, right? I just told you that we have absolutely no need to have this conversation with you. We know more about what you've done and why than you do. Xi De, the tight structure of the new world is not what you or the average person imagines it to be. If you can calmly go about your business and not cause problems, the day will come when you can rise to a position like mine. At that time, you'll understand everything, including the secrets of power, the meaning of life, and the beautiful future of mankind. Xi De, assure us, the policy makers, so that we can have an easy conscience and overlook the existence of the three hundred workers from the Steel-Cutting Plant as well as your strange ideas about aliens from outer space invading the earth. It's all nonsense. In the year before you were born, the Supreme Committee announced an unprecedented plan. The plan was called Zero, and its object was to make humankind evolve into a genuinely higher species. It sounds like a legend, but has been extremely successful in the last thirty years. The plan aims to eliminate 10 percent of the inferior population every ten years. These people are short-lived and work less effectively than machines. Their greatest crime is being completely unaware that humanity is evolving. Our biochemistry labs have made surprising breakthroughs in the last few years and have figured out that humans can be made immortal, which means that the earth will be ruled by a group of carefully chosen, wise, and immortal people. And because they are immortal, there will be an unlimited amount of time for study, by which eventually society will be made classless. That will be the first truly egalitarian society in history. Humanity will sit on jeweled thrones like the gods ruling over obedient machines. No longer will we be like the lower animals, continuing to exist through subsequent generations. We will be our own descendants, an unending generation. We will be eternal like God and the new world our Heaven. We will be able to sow this happiness on less developed planets. We will become the seed carriers of the universe, driving our chariots of the sun, traveling amid the stars for all eternity."

Xi De looked with surprise at the assistant director's face, which had grown flushed with excitement. After a while, Xi De couldn't help but ask one more question.

"But why did you come for me?"

"When you were born, our labs invented an 'auxiliary thought device' that could be implanted in the brain. This small, unusual crystal is capable of receiving and recording information from and transmitting information to your brain. We were extremely excited about this, believing that in addition to exercising complete control over the thought of human beings in the future, we would also be able to educate them. Therefore we began by implanting the crystals in the brains of infants because there was less chance of an infant rejecting them than an adult. Soon after, however, we discovered that their effectiveness was less than we anticipated. The infants died young; you were the only exception. Ultimately, we halted the experiment. We handed you and these devices over to a group of psychologists who would conduct research dealing with the subconscious, reason, and judgment. Utilizing this auxiliary thought device, they allowed you from a very young age to experience these two contradictory frames of mind: the highly scientific civilization in which you found yourself and the old vanished world of the soul. On account of this, you naturally developed an interest in history while having doubts about the system of the new world. After you graduated and joined the Resource Analysis Bureau, the psychologists gave you a greater shock: they summoned you to read Winston's book *The True Face of the Supreme Committee*. Xi De, do you recall the three successive days of strange images? That had absolutely nothing to do with superspiritual phenomena."

"What!" Xi De wanted to leap out of his chair, but restrained himself. He kept telling himself that all this was the dirty tricks of the aliens. The information obtained while he was under hypnosis had been used to fabricate this story. It had to be a trap laid by the aliens, a frightful and evil trap.

"Xi De," said the assistant director in a loud voice, "don't you get it now?"

Excited, Xi De looked up at that face.

"I don't believe any of it. I don't believe a single word of what you've said."

The room grew silent, and the face on the screen recovered its deathly gray pallor.

After a long while, the assistant director heaved a long sigh.

"Xi De, why can't I convince you?"

"You can deal with me in any number of ways, but you will never trick me."

"So you still think I'm an alien?"

"Yes, that's exactly what you are," Xi De suddenly shouted. "You're a disgusting alien with no shame. You plan to gradually eliminate us. You created us, you created civilization, but you have no right to destroy your creation. You can't treat us like rats in a lab—you have no right to—you can't end it like that with a pat on the backside."

The face gradually faded away as he shouted. The wall took on its original appearance and the lights came on in the room again, as if nothing had happened. Xi De sat alone on the sofa in the middle of the empty room, holding his head and weeping. It was the heartrending wail only an organism entirely without hope could make.

27

"This is probably the last one for today," said the guy sitting at the control panel to the guy standing next to him. "We've had to do a lot of them recently."

The guy standing grunted as he turned to look at the tightly sealed steel-gray metallic room.

"I gotta get a new job," said the guy sitting. "Vaporizing people every day is really boring."

"Okay," said the guy standing, "release the vapor and open the door."

After the door opened, he stepped into the vaporization chamber. He came back out with a small metal tag in his hand.

"AH5481," he read softly. "AH5481—hey, that's a central official!"

Translated by John Balcom